FAIR EXCHANGE IS ROBBERY

Recent Titles by Jeffrey Ashford from Severn House

THE COST OF INNOCENCE
FAIR EXCHANGE IS ROBBERY
AN HONEST BETRAYAL
LOOKING-GLASS JUSTICE
MURDER WILL OUT
A TRUTHFUL INJUSTICE
A WEB OF CIRCUMSTANCES

Writing as Roderic Jeffries

DEFINITELY DECEASED
SEEING IS DECEIVING
AN INTRIGUING MURDER

FAIR EXCHANGE IS ROBBERY

Jeffrey Ashford

This first world edition published in Great Britain 2003 by
SEVERN HOUSE PUBLISHERS LTD of
9–15 High Street, Sutton, Surrey SM1 1DF.
This first world edition published in the USA 2003 by
SEVERN HOUSE PUBLISHERS INC of
595 Madison Avenue, New York, N.Y. 10022.

British Library Cataloguing in Publication Data

Ashford, Jeffrey, 1926–
    Fair exchange is robbery
    1. Kidnapping - Fiction
    2. Detective and mystery stories
    I. Title
    823.9'14 [F]

ISBN 0-7278-5972-2

Typeset by Palimpsest Book Production Ltd.,
Polmont, Stirlingshire, Scotland.
Printed and bound in Great Britain by
MPG Books Ltd., Bodmin, Cornwall.

One

Penfold switched off the computer, leaned back in the chair and stared at the VDU screen as it showed a final circle of light and then became blank. Several weeks ago he had advised Boris, one of the shuttlecocks – as department managers were known because of their ability to change their opinions in tune with the board at head office – that he had discovered a fault in security which meant a really clever hacker could break into a large number of the files and it was necessary to devise a further and stronger defence. Should he start work on that? He'd never received an answer. Boris might not have reported his warning to the board. If time were spent on modifying the existing system, a proposed new network could almost certainly not be designed and installed on time; it was company policy that, after a project had been prepared, accepted, costed and timed, any delay would adversely affect bonuses. Boris loved money. Everyone needed someone or something to love and he was married to Enid . . .

Sometimes, he thought as he stood, he almost agreed with Lucy that he was a survivor from the past. The previous week he'd been in London, and when on the tube between Oxford Circus and Tottenham Court Road, he had offered his seat to a lady with orange and green hair, who had looked ill. She had sneeringly said she didn't need no favours from a poncy hopeful. On reflection, she had not been ill, merely made up in modern style. Boris would not have been so misled. Boris was with it. He maintained that one owed no sense of loyalty to employers, because they would make one redundant without a second's hesitation.

He left the desk, the other six of which had long since been deserted because there was no extra pay for overtime, and crossed to the coat-stand, lifted off his mackintosh. He made his way along the corridor to the lifts. On the ground floor, there was no security guard at the control desk in the atrium. Convinced no one else remained in the building, was he brewing himself a cup of tea? It was raining, and Penfold put on his mackintosh before leaving by the small door, now in one-way mode, to the side of the main entrance. There was a forty-yard walk to the underground car park and by the time he reached its cover, his hair was wet enough for him to brush the moisture off with his hand. Originally, there had been direct inside access to the car park, but this had been cut in the name of security. No one's bonus had been threatened by the implementation of this measure.

His Jaguar and the security guard's Rover were the only cars remaining, and as he approached it, he enjoyed the satisfaction of success. Pride was one of the deadly sins, but if one sinned a little, it made one's virtues that much more admirable. His parents had been rich in warmth, but poor in financial acumen owing to his father's firm belief that the *raison d'être* for money was its spending. A comfortable childhood and early teens had been followed by hard times . . . He pressed the remote button on the key and the car doors unlocked. He settled behind the wheel, put the key into the ignition, but did not immediately start the engine. Lucy sometimes teased him over his pride of possession. She had never gone without. Her parents had not been all that wealthy, but had always enjoyed a very comfortable lifestyle because they had recognized that a pound spent today could not be spent tomorrow.

He'd met her at a dance. For much of the evening, they'd been together and for him the world had taken on a golden glow which had dimmed a little when he'd escorted her to her BMW – his car was an ancient Ford, well past its pensionable age.

He'd phoned her some days later.

'Yes,' a woman had said.

Tone and abrupt manner had painted a mental picture of Lucy's mother as tall, thin and toothy, with all the warmth of a hungry crocodile. 'Can I speak to Lucy, please?'

'Who are you?'

Whoever he was, it seemed he was not welcome. 'Gavin Penfold,' he'd admitted.

'Who?'

He'd repeated his name.

There was a silence. He'd imagined her marching into a large drawing room filled with antiques and family portraits, telling Lucy that some little man was on the phone and would she like to be out?

'Hullo, Gavin.'

'I hope you remember me . . .'

She'd laughed. Even over the line, it was music. 'What an extraordinary thing to say! Did I seem that scatter-brained?'

'Of course not, but . . .' Some things were better left unexplained. 'I was hoping you'd have a meal with me at one of the local restaurants.'

'Not if it's the Red Barn. The last time I was there, they added a small snail to my tuna salad.'

'But if we try somewhere else . . . ?'

'I'd like that.'

'When are you free?'

'My social calendar isn't bursting at the seams.'

He'd been surprised. 'How about tomorrow?'

'Fine.'

'I'll pick you up at around eight?'

'Get here at seven and we'll have a drink.'

When he'd rung off, a choir had been singing. One didn't have to be in one's teens to suffer the insanity a woman could provoke.

The drawing room at Alton House was large, but not filled with priceless antiques, and there were no heavily framed portraits on the walls; her mother was not tall, skinny, buck-toothed and bitchy – she just disliked speaking on the phone; her father was cheerfully friendly.

Several months later, he'd nervously asked Lucy to marry him. She'd replied that it had taken him an unflatteringly long time to ask her. Her parents had expressed their pleasure at the news of the engagement, and when he had begun to explain that, because he was still relatively work-inexperienced, it would be some time before he could provide Lucy with all he wanted to . . . her mother had stopped him. Whatever home he provided, if it was filled with love and happiness, that was all that mattered.

He'd worked very hard, spent a considerable sum of money on taking specialized courses to increase and expand his skills; he'd become a licensed hacker, and the man who had trained him had remarked that in the face of his skills, actual and intuitive, no security system was a hundred per cent safe; he'd changed employers, each time climbing up the ladder. Success had enabled them to move (thanks to a heavy mortgage) from a small, rather ugly Victorian house in south Pettersgrove to a beautiful fifteenth-century manor house in Fieldhurst. And he'd bought a Jaguar . . .

The past vanished. As he went to turn the ignition key, his coat sleeve rose sufficiently for him to see his watch. Lucy was used to his irregular homecomings, but even so, she might well be starting to worry by now. He reached down to his coat pocket for his mobile, failed to find it and remembered he'd left it on his desk. He decided to drive home rather than take the time to retrieve it.

He started the engine, backed a few yards, turned and drove up to the ramp, used the remote control to activate the security gate. The rain was still moderately heavy; it was to be hoped the weather would improve if they spent a weekend with the Morgans in East Sussex. Giles, Ronda and the twins were a family with an anarchic attitude towards life – in their company, the mental cobwebs which came from sitting in front of a VDU for hours or mentally designing networks were blown away.

As he breasted Castle Hill, the lights turned red and he braked to a halt. There had never been a recorded castle within miles of Pettersgrove, but the name added a suggestion of cachet to a town which needed all it could get. In the past fifty years, it had lost the little character it had once possessed; the market had disappeared, as had every family-owned shop in High Street, and local development planning had typically ensured that those properties which should have been preserved had not been, those that should not, had.

The lights changed and he turned right, to drive past the railway station and along roads lined by terrace houses to the countryside. Some years before, the board of the Counties Bank had decided to move Security out of the City in the name of economy – an economy which had not extended to their own salaries and bonuses. The majority of the staff at that time had been opposed to the move; he welcomed it, since it enabled him to live in a house surrounded by hedges, fields and woods without suffering hours of commuting. He didn't know why he had so strong a love of the countryside. His parents, grandparents and great-grandparents had all been townspeople. Perhaps further back there was an ancestor who had ploughed, sowed, reaped, stooked, threshed, and it was his genes that had galloped ahead of competitors.

Headlights marked a car which was coming up the side road ahead to his left. Knowing the driver would face a 'Stop' sign, he did not slacken speed and was totally unprepared for the car's coming out immediately ahead of him. He braked fiercely, felt the back wheels begin to skid on the wet road, managed to kill the skid as much by luck as skill. He swore and asked the night whether the other driver was drunk or crazy? As the car, which he now identified as a Saab, slowed, forcing him to do the same, he decided both. He depressed the indicator stalk and began to draw out to overtake. The Saab drifted across the road, blocking his path.

A car came up behind and closed, lights undipped, and the glare made him squint and alter the rear-view mirror to dim mode. A drunk crazy in front, a selfish fool behind . . . A few hundred yards further on, there was a turning to the right which would take him home on a longer, roundabout route, but one he could hope to make in safety. He made the mistake of indicating his intention. The Saab slowed still more and he was forced to brake again; the car behind closed to box him in. Too late, he realized he was the victim of drivers who were skilfully working together.

They forced him to stop. An oncoming car approached and now, as scared as previously he had been annoyed, with ridiculous futility he shouted for help as he flashed the headlights. The car passed, the driver concentrating on reaching home quickly. The Jaguar's driving door was opened by a man who wore a ski-mask.

'Out.'

He fought panic. A recent programme on television had featured a victim of carjacking who had tried to fight back and been severely stabbed – a detective sergeant had told viewers they should remember that there wasn't a car worth a knife in the guts. He said, mouth dry, voice shaky: 'I'll give you—'

The man, with a violence that shocked, grabbed his coat collar and hauled him out of the driving seat and on to the road.

'D'you want money?'

A blow to the stomach caused him to double up. As he gagged, desperately trying to draw breath into his lungs, his mouth, hands and feet were secured with masking tape, and a ski-mask was pulled over his head, cutting out all light except for what little filtered through the close weave. With more careless force, he was thrust into the back of the Jaguar and wedged into the well between front and back seats.

Car doors were slammed shut. The Jaguar drove forward, accelerating fiercely.

'Lovely job, eh, Bert?'

'Yeah.'

'Jags are racing again.'

'You don't tell.'

'Back in the old days, they was always winning at Le Mans. Nothing could touch 'em.' The driver spoke enthusiastically and at very considerable length, despite the derisory remarks, about the Jaguar victories in the fifties, the development of the sports cars, the company's return to racing . . .

'Shit!'

'What's up?'

'I must of missed a turning some time back.'

'Because you were too busy talking crap.' Bert swore at length, but without variety. 'So why go on, you bleeding berk – turn round and get back to where you went wrong.'

'There's no need – I can find the way cross-country.'

Moments later, Bert said: 'Cool it, you mad sod.'

'You think this is fast?' Al laughed. 'You ain't no bottle.'

'And you ain't George Friedland.'

'He's a biker not a racing driver.'

Their speed increased.

'Slow it or you'll have a sodding blue on our tail.'

'I could lose any of them in the first quarter-mile.'

'Can't you bloody see there's a village coming up?'

'So keep your muscles tight.'

'Get picked up for speeding and Reg'll pull your thick head through your ring.'

'I could take this corner faster'n Stirling ever could . . .'

The car swung violently as Penfold heard a muted thud.

'Jesus, you hit her!'

'She came out so sudden . . .'

7

Bert cursed him, pausing only long enough to demand what Ed could see through the back window.

'She's flat out and ain't moving.'

'Is there anyone else?'

'No . . . Yes. A woman on the other side, looking.'

'Can she read the number?'

'How the sod would I know?'

They went around another, gentler corner at greatly reduced speed.

'There weren't nothing I could do. She came out so sudden . . .'

'And you was driving like you was on the track . . . I've got to bell Reg on the mobile and give the word.'

'There ain't no need for that.'

'A six-inch plank ain't your thick.'

'I don't think . . .'

'Dead right, you don't. Now belt up while I talk to Reg . . . Reg, there's been a problem . . . No, he's here . . . It's like this. Al was driving a bit quick, like—'

'No, I weren't,' Al shouted. 'The stupid bitch never looked and . . .' Concentrating on denial rather than his driving, he let the car swerve and the nearside wheel mounted the grass verge. Swearing, he regained control.

'I wasn't saying nothing, Reg, because we just near ended up in the ditch,' Bert said. 'He was driving too sodding fast and when we was going through the village, he hit a broad . . . Left her lying on the road . . . There was another woman around, only she was a bit away . . . Can't say for certain, only it ain't likely . . . But . . . You want us to do what? . . . I ain't arguing, it's just . . . Sure; like you tell, Reg.'

'What's he say?' Al demanded.

'That he'll feed bits of you to his carp . . . Drive back to the town and find a twenty-four-hour supermarket.'

'Talk straight. We need out as fast as we can bleeding well move.'

'And when we're there, you'll buy a litre bottle of whisky.'

'He thinks I'm stopping outside a supermarket in a car the coppers could be wanting to eyeball?'

'You like to use the mobile to tell Reg you ain't doing as he says?'

Al did not answer.

Two

The 999 call was routed through the Operations Room in county HQ. The WPC prepared to calm the caller, but quickly discovered she would not need to do so. Mrs Fenella Gill was clearly not of an hysterical nature. Had an ambulance been called? Before the present call. Then would Mrs Gill describe what had happened? . . .

Walking home, after visiting a sick friend in Trenton Street, she had been approaching the sharp corner in Houghton Road as someone had stepped off the pavement to cross the road. A car had come round the corner very quickly, knocked the woman down and driven on.

The WPC asked, with little hope of an affirmative answer, if Mrs Gill had been able to note the car's registration number? Naturally, she had tried to read it. The first two letters had been RA, the two figures 02, the next two letters FU, but she'd been unable to make out the last letter because by then the car had been some way away and her eyesight was not as good as it had once been. And the car was a Jaguar. Hiding her disbelief, the WPC asked how she could be so certain? An acquaintance owned one and so she knew what they looked like . . .

After noting Mrs Gill's address and explaining that a police officer would be along as soon as possible to take a written statement, the WPC tactfully brought the call to an end. She rang E division and reported the incident, adding that an ambulance had been called; she activated the computer terminal in front of her and requested a vehicle identification, RA 02 FU?, possibly a Jaguar.

She picked up her notes, walked across to the duty inspector who sat at a desk near to the very large-scale county map which hung on the wall. 'Hit-and-run in Oak Cross, female victim, condition not yet known, sir,' she said, as she handed the paper across.

The inspector read, his head bent at an angle that caused his thick neck to form flesh folds. 'Not·thought to request a vehicle identification?' he said with sarcastic certainty. In his book, women police officers were only good for one thing, and many of them not even that.

'I've put it through,' she answered.

'Informed the division?'

'Yes.'

'Entered your log?'

'Not yet.'

'Seems like I even need to remind you to blow your nose.'

'Knowing you, it'll be something else you want blown. Sir.'

He silently swore as she walked away. He'd once tried to get his hands under her skirt and she'd brushed them away with the insulting suggestion that, at his age and in his condition, it would not be an uplifting experience.

The Jaguar drove into the supermarket's forecourt and came to a stop at the far end of the parking lines. Al was ordered to buy a bottle of Scotch. Reluctantly, he climbed out of the car and crossed to the building.

Ed said, 'He's dead right, you know.'

'Yeah?' Bert muttered.

'With us sitting here, like bleeding rabbits.'

'It's doing what Reg said.'

'So what's with him? Don't he realize the blues'll be looking for this car if that woman sussed the number?'

'Forget it.'

'But if she did . . . ?'

'Reg knows what he's doing.'

'It ain't him having to do, it's us. Buying a bottle of whisky when we're hot!'

Bert silently agreed. Even an ounce of brains said to get as far away as possible. But Reg was smart; more importantly, he didn't like his orders being ignored.

A man and a woman, the man pushing a trolley, walked up to the nearest car, four empty bays away. Their voices carried and Penfold could just make out what the woman was saying. Judy and Clive were coming to dinner in two days' time and they'd really enjoy a leg of lamb. But was the wine good enough, since Clive knew so much about it? Clive, the man said, was full of bull and likely couldn't tell a decent wine from plonk and this bottle had cost almost eight quid, so if he didn't like it, he could . . .

Their conversation, which came from a mundane world, exacerbated Penfold's fears to the point where he panicked and he struggled to raise himself out of the well in order to gain the attention of the couple.

Something cold touched the side of his neck.

'Relax or you're sodding dead.'

He slumped back, now, because of overwhelming helplessness, doubly conscious of the pain of his contorted posture. The knife was removed.

Al returned, pulled open the driving door. 'Is there any movement?' he asked anxiously, as he sat behind the wheel.

'A couple of coppers are checking cars on the far side.'

'Then let's get moving,' he said wildly as he dropped the plastic bag and bottle on Bert's lap, and started the engine.

Their jeering laughter made him curse.

The lay-by – the old road before the corner had been reduced to a mild curve – was three hundred yards long and edged by a screen of unkempt bushes, overgrown weeds and grass, and a couple of ancient oaks. Two plastic rubbish bins had been set up; naturally, these were half-empty, but surrounded by litter.

Bert stepped out of the Jaguar. 'Get him out.'

Penfold was dragged out of the car with the same careless disregard of injury as when he had been forced into the well.

'Get the whisky.'

Ed brought the bottle out of the car.

'Raise the mask so as he can drink, but keep his eyes bunged.'

The ski-mask was rolled up above Penfold's mouth, the tape ripped off with painful force.

'Open the bottle and get him drinking.'

Ed unscrewed the cap of the bottle, threw it away, raised the neck of the bottle to Penfold's mouth. Penfold pressed his lips together. His hair was gripped and his head drawn back, the bottle forced between lips and teeth. Whisky flowed into his mouth. He swallowed, gagged, choked.

'You're not trying to drown him, you stupid bastard.'

Whisky, at a much lesser rate, flowed once more. After a while, he suffered a feeling of nausea, complemented by growing mental confusion . . .

'Shove him in the front.'

He was thrown forward with a force than sent him crashing into the car. His shoulder was gripped and he was swung round and manhandled on to the front passenger seat.

'Get his dabs on this.'

His right hand was seized and his fingers pressed down on the bottle; he didn't wonder why – he was beyond caring why.

He collapsed to his right, knocking his head against the steering wheel; he sprawled across the driving seat, was roughly pushed upright; he slumped against the door.

'Shove the bottle on the floor.'

He desperately called on the world to stop spinning . . .
He vomited. He was cursed with vicious crudity.

The car moved and he vomited again. The cursing resumed. After a while, the car stopped. He was dragged across to the driving seat and his head hit something that he vaguely thought was probably the steering wheel. The world spun away . . .

He was conscious of a woman's voice.

'Gavin, what's the matter? Are you ill?'

He thought he ought to know who was asking the questions.

'Oh God, darling, is it your heart?' The driving door was flung open. 'You . . . you're not ill; you've been drinking!'

He tried to explain, but his tongue was on strike and he could only mumble incoherently.

'How could you be so damned stupid?'

He looked up at a woman whose heads merged and separated.

'Go into the house, strip off all your clothes, and for God's sake have a bath. I'll put what I can in the washing machine, but your suit will have to go to the cleaners. Have you any idea how revolting you smell and look?'

He giggled because the woman was Lucy, yet it had taken him all this time to recognize her.

'Will you get out of the car?'

Legs tried to refuse to do what he wanted, but eventually he managed to climb out of the car. He would have collapsed to the ground had she not hurried to support him.

'Now *I'm* damned well going to have to have a bath as well!'

She continued to support him on the interminable, immensely difficult task of walking up to and through the garden gateway, around the corner of the house, through the front doorway and into the hall.

'Take your clothes off down here.'

He didn't move.

'Shakespeare should have added an eighth age,' she said, as she struggled to pull off his jacket, ' – mewling and puking in his wife's arms.'

He fuzzily wondered who Shakespeare was.

Three

'When I was your age,' Myers said, as he looked up at Kendrick, who stood by his desk, 'nick someone and it was five minutes' paperwork; now it's an hour when you're lucky.'

Did Myers ever really consider himself lucky? Kendrick wondered. Furrowed forehead, square face, broad nostrils and aggressive set to thick lips surely marked someone who believed his life had been blackballed at birth.

'Last year the Home Secretary said he was going to cut red tape so the police could do what they're supposed to: bust crime. Didn't cut nothing. Since then, every time we bang up chummy, there's more forms than ever to be filled in. All the politicians are good at is passing laws that make things easier for the villains and bollocking us when the clear-up rate goes down as a result.'

The phone on the next desk rang.

'Well, are you going to go on standing there?'

Kendrick crossed to the next desk, yet again resentful at the way in which Myers, who was 'puppy-walking' him as an introduction to the workings of CID, treated him more as a skivvy than an aide. He lifted the receiver. A detective sergeant from E division started to make a report; he asked the other to wait, picked up the phone, which was on a very long lead, and handed it to Myers.

Myers listened, said they were too busy . . . 'All right, all right, no need to start pulling rank . . . Yeah, I'll get back.' He slammed the receiver down. 'Couldn't wait another half-hour, could they?'

'For what?'

'To let the night shift come on and have to respond.'

'What's the play?'

'Some woman's been knocked down in Oak Cross by a hit-and-run and there's a vehicle identification to confirm.'

'Why us, since Oak Cross isn't in our patch . . . ?'

'Gawd! You've left your brains at home. The car's been logged to someone in our division, so we've got to get a butcher's at it.'

'Will that take long?'

'How the hell should I know?'

'It's just . . . I'm meeting Margery as soon as this shift ends.'

'You were.'

'But when I had to call off only the other day and couldn't let her know in time, she gave me real hell . . . Dave, you could manage without me, couldn't you?'

'Nothing easier.'

'That's great. Then I'll . . .'

'Only I'm not going to because I've been ordered to turn you into a detective by someone who doesn't realize that's impossible.' He stood. 'Let's move.'

Miserable sod! Kendrick thought. 'Then I'll have to give Margery a bell to say I can't make it.'

'Forget that. There's not the time.'

He reached across the desk, lifted the receiver and dialled. Margaret's mother answered, so he took the coward's route and asked her to pass on the message that he was terribly sorry, he couldn't meet Margaret as arranged because unexpected work had turned up and he'd be in touch again as soon as he knew what was what. He was reasonably certain Mrs Tennant would be content to pass on the message since she'd recently made it clear that she did not presume Margery and he spent their time in mind-improving discussion when he saw her after a late turn. Mothers always suspected the

17

worst. Probably the memory of their own youths fuelled their suspicions.

'Would his lordship be ready to leave?' Myers asked, with lead-weighted sarcasm.

Twenty minutes later, as the drizzle finally ceased, they turned into the entrance yard, bordered on one side by a garage and a large shed, on the other by a small orchard. A silver Jaguar was parked very untidily in front of the right-hand, open half of the garage, and the Fiesta's headlights raised quick flashes from the raindrops on the bodywork.

'Looks promising,' Myers said, as he braked to a halt. 'So now you can tell me what we do.'

'Find out if Mr or Mrs Penfold was driving it this evening.'

'You don't think it might first be best to see if the registration number matches the crime report?'

'I was taking that as read.'

'Only it wasn't, was it? And shall I tell you why? It was because you were thinking of nookie, not work . . . So what after that?'

'We question the Penfolds to find out if one or both of them—'

'We make a visual search of the car before they learn they've been eyeballed and try to clean off the evidence. Have you ever considered becoming a roadsweeper?'

'Can't say I have.'

'Then reviewing your talents as a detective, I'd say, start considering.' Myers released his seat belt, reached into the door pocket for a torch, opened the door, climbed out, checked the registration number. 'Bingo!' Followed by Kendrick, he slowly walked anticlockwise around the car, shining the torch up and down, and came to a halt in front of the nearside headlamp. 'Take a look.' As he finished speaking, an outside house light was switched on.

He shone the torch on the top half of the headlight and Kendrick saw a short length of thread which had been caught up in the rim. 'Does that say anything to you?'

'It could have come from the victim's clothes and been wedged there at the time of impact.'

'Well, well, faint glimmerings of intelligence! If there was contact at that point, what might then have happened?'

'She could have been thrown up and backwards, leaving an impression on the paintwork of the bonnet.'

'The lad's in danger of becoming useful.' Myers leaned over the bonnet and played the beam backwards and forwards. He straightened up. 'I'd say there's something, but the water's making it difficult to be certain and it'll need Vehicles to—'

He was interrupted by a call from the garden. 'Who are you? What are you doing?'

'Police.' He said to Kendrick: 'Show her your ID – if you've remembered to carry it?'

Kendrick crunched his way along the gravel yard to a four-foot-high wooden gate, set in a thorn hedge, beyond which stood a woman, a mobile in her right hand. He held his warrant card open, making certain it was well illuminated by the overhead light. 'PC Kendrick, county police. And DC Myers is by the car . . . Are you Mrs Penfold?'

'What are you doing?' she demanded a second time.

'We've been asked to examine the Jaguar in the yard.'

'Why?'

'It'll be best if my companion explains.'

She hesitated, turned suddenly and walked round the corner of the house and out of sight.

He returned to the Jaguar. Myers stood by the opened driving door, and as he approached, said, 'The answer to all the questions.' He shone the torch inside the car.

Kendrick smelled the vomit before he saw it on the front seat, dashboard, steering wheel, and in the well.

'That was Mrs Penfold?'

'Yes.' He stepped back, glad to escape the stench.

'Then it's a fiver to a broken button it's a husband or a

boyfriend who, pissed as a newt, knocked the woman down. So let's go in and find out which.' He shut the car door and started walking, the swing of his arm causing the torch beam to sweep the gravel. 'You let me do all the talking inside. This place says money, so I don't want you being stupid and ballsing things up.' Two paces further on, he said, 'It's big, old, and in the country. There wouldn't be change from a million plus quid to buy it. Not for the likes of us, that's for bloody sure.'

Kendrick didn't begrudge the Penfolds their home, as Myers so obviously did. Myers was forever inveighing against the inequalities of wealth, but of one thing he was certain: were Myers ever to become wealthy, he would cease to be troubled by any of them.

Lucy opened the heavy wooden front door as they approached and they stepped into a beamed hall in which were a few pieces of furniture, each of some note: a seventeenth-century oak coffer, two heavily carved wainscot chairs, a credence table with fold-over top . . .

'We'll go in here,' she said, as she pulled on the leather thong which activated a holding bar on the interior of the panelled door.

The sitting room, heavily beamed, with a large inglenook fireplace in which logs burned in a wrought-iron basket, was furnished for comfort rather than period; colour was provided by the curtains and the Kazak carpet of intricate design in reds, yellows, browns, blues, black and white.

'Do sit.'

They settled on comfortable armchairs.

'May I offer you something? Coffee or a drink?'

'Not for us,' Myers said gracelessly.

Myers, Kendrick was certain, resentfully misjudged her manner as condescending. She was older than he had first judged when she had been outside and partly in shadow. Wavy brown hair, blue eyes, a pert nose, a generous mouth shaped for smiling, and a soft, smooth complexion combined to form an attractive face in which there was considerable character.

'Perhaps you'd now like to explain what it is you want?' she said.

Myers answered. 'There's been an accident in Oak Cross: a woman was knocked down by a car. . .'

'I'm very sorry to hear that. Was she badly hurt?'

'She was taken to hospital, but I can't say any more for the moment . . . The car did not stop and so we're trying to identify it.'

'Then why come here?'

'An eyewitness was able to determine almost all the registration number of the car, which leads us to believe it might have been the Jaguar that is now standing outside the garage here.'

She stared at Myers for several seconds and her shocked concern was obvious. 'That's utterly ridiculous!' she said forcefully, as she looked away.

'The Jaguar out there is your car?'

'My husband's.'

'Is he here?'

'He's ill and in bed.'

'Has he been there all day?'

'Only since returning from work.'

'He's suffering from a very sudden illness, then?' Myers said, only just not sneering.

Her lips tightened.

'Why didn't he drive the car into the garage?'

'I've just told you: he was taken ill.'

'On the journey?'

She didn't answer.

'What time did he return home?'

'I didn't notice.'

'You'll have some idea of when it was.'

Her voice sharpened. 'You are in the habit of telling people what they do or don't notice?'

In turn, Myers's manner openly changed. 'Is there a reason for you not remembering?'

'Are you trying to insinuate something?'

'As I have already said, there is reason to believe it was your husband's car that struck the victim.'

'You also said the eyewitness did not read all the registration number. Then there can't be a positive identification and it is outrageous you should accuse my husband of having been the driver.'

'I will explain in greater detail, Mrs Penfold,' Myers said, enjoying himself. 'It was only the last letter of the final three which the eyewitness was unable to read and since four letters of the alphabet were not used because they would have formed unsuitable combinations, the number of possible cars is reduced to twenty-two.'

'But you're still ready to come here—'

'The eyewitness identified the car in question as a Jaguar and only one of the twenty-two is of that make.'

She tried to argue further. 'Then it's obvious her identification was wrong.'

'When we arrived, I briefly examined the Jaguar standing outside the garage. Caught on the nearside headlamp is a thread of material.'

'Well?'

'When a vehicle incident involves a pedestrian or cyclist, some part of the victim's clothing is often caught in the vehicle's bodywork.'

'The thread must have come from what I was wearing when I brushed the headlamp.'

'Another fact, Mrs Penfold: when a body is struck by a car, it is frequently thrown up and backwards and a pattern of the victim's clothing is recorded on the car's paintwork. I think there is such a pattern on the Jaguar's bonnet.'

'If so, it will have come from one of the times when I've sat on the bonnet.'

'That hardly seems likely.'

'You've never followed the hunt or been to a point-to-point?'

He had done neither and saw her words as a social criticism rather than a question. 'Scientific tests will prove whether the thread and pattern came from the victim's clothes.'

'And bring your unwelcome observations to an end.'

'There is an empty whisky bottle in the front well of the Jaguar.'

'What are you now trying to suggest?'

'That your husband may well have drunk the contents.'

'He does not like whisky.'

'Yet perhaps he managed to overcome his dislike?'

'I think I've heard enough . . .'

'There is vomit over the interior of the front of the Jaguar.'

'As I told you, my husband was taken ill.'

'On the drive back here? You have not mentioned seeking medical attention. Why not? Was it because you could judge his illness was due to his having drunk too much?'

'I judged no such thing.'

'Mrs Penfold, I should like to question your husband.'

'Out of the question.'

'Then I'll put it in a different way. I intend to question your husband.'

'In my house, I decide what you may or may not do.'

'It appears there may be sufficient evidence to charge him on suspicion of driving when under the influence of alcohol or drugs.'

'Are you now ridiculously accusing him of taking cocaine?'

'Of driving when under the influence, of being involved in a collision with a pedestrian who suffered injuries, the extent of which are not yet known, and of not stopping after the accident and reporting it. Do I speak to him and offer him the chance to refute the evidence?'

'You can return tomorrow when he may be better and able to reply to this nonsense.'

'I must speak to him now. And surely, if I decide it necessary he be medically examined, you would appreciate that?'

She stared at him, dislike and fear hardening her expression, and said in a low voice, 'You're a . . .' She stopped abruptly.

Bastard? Kendrick silently suggested.

'Shall we come with you so that if Mr Penfold is still very weak, it will save him having to move?' Myers asked, mocking her with his apparent thoughtfulness.

She ignored him, crossed to the door and went out into the hall. They followed her up the staircase, with heavy, carved balusters, and along a richly carpeted corridor. She opened the last right-hand door, went into the bedroom.

Penfold lay awkwardly on the bed, the bedclothes partially drawn back. His eyes were shut, his breathing heavy and noisy, his complexion pallid. By the side of the bed was a bucket and from this came the acrid smell of vomit.

'Mr Penfold,' Myers said. He repeated the name. He moved forward and shook Penfold, whose only response was brief, slurred mumbling.

'I will have to ask a doctor to confirm the cause of your husband's condition. Perhaps you'll be kind enough to allow us to use your telephone to call him?'

Myers would have stood as close to the guillotine as he could get, Kendrick thought.

The doctor, a local GP, one of the three certified to carry out police work, completed his examination. 'There's little doubt his condition is due to very heavy drinking; indeed, to begin with, I thought it might be necessary to have him taken to hospital, but I now judge that not to be so.'

'Then we need a blood sample, since we can't breathalyse him,' Myers said.

'You're not doing that when he's in this state,' Lucy said wildly.

'The law allows a blood sample to be taken without a

person's consent in circumstances where there is very good reason to believe he has been driving and has been involved in an incident in which a person received injuries, and he is incapable of giving his consent.'

'I don't care what the law says.'

'I'm very sorry, Mrs Penfold,' the doctor, a man who had not lost a sense of compassion even after thirty years as a GP, said, 'but I am obliged to take a sample of blood from your husband. Perhaps you'd rather leave?'

She turned away to hide her face.

The doctor withdrew a sample of blood, which he divided between two phials. After these had been labelled and both he and Myers had initialled the label, noting identity, date and time, on each, Myers held out one. 'This is yours.'

'I don't want it,' Lucy replied.

'You should give it to your lawyer in the hope it helps persuade the jury your husband was not blind drunk when he ran down the woman.'

'Mrs Penfold should be grateful you will not be on the jury,' the doctor sharply observed.

Myers led the way out of the house, and as he went through the garden gateway, said, 'There's one stuck-up bitch!'

'You . . .' Kendrick cut short what he had been about to say.

'I what?'

'Nothing.'

'Feeling sorry for her, are you?'

'In a way.'

'Never mind some woman's lying in hospital because that drunken bastard ploughed into her?'

'But was that a good reason for giving her so rough a time when she was obviously shocked?'

'I suppose you reckon I ought to have treated her with kid gloves just because she lives in a big house and talks toffee?'

They reached their car.

'What do we do now, Sherlock?' Myers asked.

'Phone Vehicles and tell them to send out a low-loader to collect the Jaguar.'

'And?'

'That's it.'

'Because you're in such a hurry to get your leg over?'

'Margery . . .' Once again, Kendrick did not finish the sentence. Myers would only jeer if he knew that he and Margery might *explore*, but had decided not to arrive at the destination before they were married.

'You don't think it might be an idea to use tape to secure the thread, to cover the impression on the bonnet with plastic, to bag the empty bottle – because if all that's not done, the lads from Vehicles are so bloody ham-fisted there'd be no evidence left?'

Kendrick gloomily thought how much more pleasant his job would have been had one of the other DCs been his mentor.

Four

Penfold was conscious of a thumping pain in his head, a foul taste in his mouth and a churning stomach. He tried to remember the past, but his mind remained a meaningless jumble. About to be sick, he rushed into the bathroom. After flushing the WC, he staggered back to bed, convinced that dying might be more pleasant than living.

Lucy entered the room, crossed to the bed and stared down at him. 'You're back, then?'

'Unfortunately. God, I feel terrible!'

'You're surprised?'

'My head's pounding.'

'You wouldn't call that normal?'

He had hoped for comforting, not bellicose words. 'What the hell's the matter?'

'You need to ask?'

'I could do with some sympathy, not antagonism.'

'That really takes the prize! I'm supposed to be sympathetic when you were so late last night that I began to worry because you hadn't phoned and when you did arrive, you were sick drunk?'

'Because I was made to drink.'

'At least that's one excuse I haven't heard before.'

'You've got to understand—'

'I did. But for my and Charles's sake, I tried to make out that you were too ill to see them. Of course, they insisted they had to talk to you, then only had to see you to realize you were dead drunk. And that poisonous man had the chance to say so

27

smugly that he was sure I'd be grateful they were calling out a doctor because he'd confirm what was wrong with you.'

'What men? What doctor?'

'You don't even remember that much? It's your lost night . . . My God! Didn't you agree to cut right back on your drinking because if you didn't, something terrible would happen? How right you were!'

'What has happened?'

She crossed to the nearer chair and sat. As she stared at him, fear overcame her anger. 'Some time after you returned last night, two detectives turned up and demanded to speak to you because a woman had been knocked down and injured by a car that didn't stop; an eyewitness had noted almost all the number and they said it matched our Jaguar. When they examined it where you'd left it, they found a thread and an impression that they believed came from the victim. They called a doctor, who took a sample of your blood even though I tried to stop it. They say . . .' She began to cry.

He suffered a sense of helplessness.

She brushed tears from her cheeks. 'They say you hit and injured her, then drove off.'

'I wasn't driving.'

She stood. 'They'll be back and probably very soon, so you'd better get up and have a bath.' She crossed to the door. 'I doubt you'll want anything to eat, but you'd better drink some coffee to help you try to pull yourself together.' She left, slamming the door behind her.

He slowly moved and sat on the edge of the bed. Once more he tried to remember. Memory moved in mists. He'd left the office late, had tried to phone her, but . . . He'd been stopped by two cars, had thought he was a victim of carjacking . . . They'd gagged and bound him, covered his head . . . The car was being driven far too quickly . . . There'd been shouting because . . . Memory cleared: because they'd hit something and now he knew that that something had been somebody . . .

28

He went through to the bathroom, shaved while the bath filled, washed, dressed in clean clothing, made his way down to the kitchen.

When she looked at him, her expression was hard.

'Are there any aspirins?' he asked.

'In the usual place.'

Clearly she was not going to get them for him, as normally she would have done had he been ill. He slowly made his way back upstairs, brain and stomach protesting at each step.

'I presumed you'd want the coffee black,' she said, as he returned to the kitchen. 'She picked up the small coffee-maker and poured out a cupful. 'The sugar's in the cupboard.'

'I don't want any, thanks.' He opened the pack of aspirins and brought out one of the foil sheets, pressed out two tablets, which he placed on the saucer. 'Let's go through to another room.'

'I'm busy.'

'We have to talk.'

'I doubt there's anything you are likely to say I want to hear.'

'I need to explain.'

'The obvious doesn't need an explanation.'

'Goddamnit, will you stop prejudging.'

'I'll tell you something, Gavin: it was only yesterday afternoon when I was in here, making a shepherd's pie for your supper, that I thought how incredibly lucky I was to be so happy. Incredible was exactly the right word.'

He went forward and put his arms around her; when she tried to break free, he held her more tightly. 'Just before we married, we promised we would always tell each other the truth. It wouldn't matter how ashamed it made one feel or even how much it might hurt. Remember?'

She did not answer, but no longer tried to break free.

'I promise I'm going to tell you the truth, however crazy it may sound. So let's go through to the other room.' He released her and waited. Without looking at him, she crossed the kitchen and left. He picked up cup and saucer and followed her into the priest's room – so named because a French Catholic priest was said to have been caught in it by two of Walsingham's spies.

He sat and drank the hot, sugarless coffee. 'I worked late last night because I wanted to finish the job, and that took longer than I expected.' He watched her, hoping the hard lines in her face would fade away. 'I drove out of the underground car park, along Chervill Street and Ingot Road, as I always do; although I didn't notice it, a car must have been following me.

'When I was approaching the Weedenhurst turning, I saw a car coming up to the main road, but knowing there was a 'Stop' sign, didn't take any notice. It drew out immediately ahead of me, causing me to brake heavily, and another car came up behind and boxed me in. When men wearing ski-masks got out, I was certain they were going to mug me and pinch the car and I tried to give them whatever they wanted, but they grabbed me, gagged and bound me, jammed a ski-mask over my head, and rammed me down into the back well of the Jaguar. The man who drove the Jaguar seemed to think he was at Silverstone. We were going around a corner far too quickly and hit someone. One of the others spoke over a mobile and then we went to an all-night supermarket, where they bought a bottle of whisky. We stopped soon afterwards in a lay-by and there they made me drink the whole bottle of whisky. I was as sick as a dog before we arrived here . . . And the rest you know. I swear that's the truth.'

'No swearing, just promising.'

'I promise that is what happened last night.'

'Why would anyone do something so terrible?'

'God knows!'

'There has to be a reason.'

He said slowly, 'You still don't believe me, do you?'

'Of course I do, when you've promised,' she said fiercely. 'It's just I'm trying to understand. That's what the detectives

are going to ask you, and if they can't or won't believe
you . . . The older detective is horrible: I'm sure he was
enjoying making me so upset. They took the Jaguar away
because he said it would prove it was your car that knocked
the woman down when you were too drunk to know what
you were doing.'

'I'll make him understand I'm telling the truth.'

'But how, when . . .'

'When it sounds so improbable?' He put an aspirin in his
mouth, drank. 'The possible takes a little time, the impossible,
a smidgen longer.' Or a bloody sight longer, he thought.

Five

K endrick read the text on the VDU, corrected a couple of literals and a spelling mistake identified with a red underline, directed the printer to print. As an aide, he had to keep a 'puppy-diary' – a report on every investigation in which he was concerned, detailing facts, evidence, the broad thrust of the enquiry, etc. Every month the diary was read by the detective inspector and criticized where necessary. It would be unusual for Ingham not to discover such necessity. He was the kind of man who would have corrected Homer . . . Unfortunately, when his time as aide was completed, it would be Ingham's assessment that would largely decide whether or not he was up to joining the CID . . . His name was called and he looked across at one of the far desks.

'Any idea where Sandy is?' Soper asked.

'No. Probably hasn't reported in yet.'

'When it's coming up to nine?'

'No one will be more surprised than he if he ever arrives for work on time.'

'He owes me a tenner and I need it like now. Don't suppose you could bridge the gap if he doesn't turn up before I have to take off?'

'How right you are.'

'If I don't buy something and get it to Viv before lunch, she'll have my guts for garters. Women get all soft over anniversaries.'

'And you've forgotten one?'

'I remembered it a couple of days ago and then it went right out of my mind. It'll be a case of the spare bedroom if I don't sneak back with something and say it's taken a long time to find because it had to be what she really wanted.'

The phone on one of the unoccupied desks rang. Kendrick stood and threaded his way between the other desks, having long since learned it was not only Myers who considered an aide to be the solution to all of life's smaller problems. He lifted the receiver. 'CID Pettersgrove.'

'Jackson, Stitchford laboratory. Re Penfold evidence. The blood analysis shows a shade over four hundred milligrams of alcohol.'

'How drunk does that make him?'

'Bordering on a coma, especially if he's not normally a heavy drinker; not very much more and he could have been closing up on medullary paralysis and maybe death. Must have been hitting the booze like there'd be no tomorrow.'

'Unfit to drive a car, then?'

'Even if it was clamped.'

Kendrick thanked the other, rang off. Using the computer, he began to write two reports giving a résumé of the evidence, one for Myers, one for his diary.

'Another one over the limit?' Soper asked.

'Over and out of sight. A little more and he could easily have died.'

'As some would say, the second most desirable way of dying . . . What's the history?'

'A woman was knocked down and quite badly injured in Oak Cross by a hit-and-run. The car's number was eyeballed and vehicle identification gave a probable, so Dave and I went along to see if we could confirm. The Jaguar showed possible signs and the owner had been as sick as a dog in it. He was in bed and too far gone to put foot to ground, so we called in the duty doctor, who took a blood sample.'

'Sounds as if the owner will be spending time inside.'

'I suppose.'

'You're not sure.'

Kendrick shrugged his shoulders.

'Reckon he'll wriggle out of it in court with a smart brief? I'd make every motorist guilty of drunk driving get out on to the roads and clean up the remains of a road-accident victim.'

Kendrick did not explain that what bothered him was memory of the wife's distress and the courageous way in which she had tried to defend her husband even though she must have recognized the futility of this. Had he tried to explain, Soper would have been scornful that he still lacked the carapace over his emotions which an effective officer had to develop.

'How's the victim now?'

'I haven't heard.'

'If I were you, I'd find out before someone asks.'

'Good thinking!' He stood, crossed to the table by the noticeboard and searched amongst the clutter until he found the local telephone directory. Back at his desk, having carried the telephone across, he dialled. A woman said she'd transfer his call to Patient Information. He had listened to *The Four Seasons* long enough for 'Spring' to have become 'Summer' before another woman told him Mrs Muriel Lynch had suffered a broken femur and severe bruising, but no internal injury; had been operated on; had regained consciousness and was in intensive care. Her condition, considering her age, was satisfactory. As he replaced the receiver, he wondered how satisfactory Muriel Lynch considered her present situation?

The door was flung open and Bonner swept in. Six foot one tall, with shoulders proportionately broad, a crooked nose broken in a rugger match, and an aggressively square chin, he considered subtlety to be a sign of wimpishness.

'You've arrived just in time,' Soper said.

'Time for what?'

'Lunch, for one thing.'

'Is anything moving?' he asked as he hung up his short overcoat.

'Yeah,' Soper replied. 'At nine fifty-six, on Saturday, the ninth of November, DC Sandy Bonner repaid the tenner he was lent yesterday to enable him to take out a skirt who'd only come across after a three-course meal and a bottle of wine.'

'And we had a second bottle and that was a best buy!' He roared with laughter as he brought a wallet out of his back trouser pocket and from it produced a ten-pound note, which he handed to Soper before continuing to his own desk.

Soper stood. 'Cover for me.' He hurried out of the room.

'What's got him concording?' Bonner asked.

'He forgot to buy his wife a present for some anniversary or other – wedding, most likely,' Kendrick answered.

'Haven't they been married long enough to forget all that nonsense?'

'You'll make a fine husband!'

'Not all the time I can run fast enough.'

Myers entered. 'The bastard!' he said, as he made his way to his desk.

'The superintendent, the chief inspector, the inspector, or the desk sergeant?' Bonner asked.

'The Guv'nor.'

'Put you down for night duty for the next six months, has he?'

He sat. 'Took him my preliminary report on the Penfold case and he told me he was taking over.'

'You're not telling us you expect to be left with anything big? Not when you've ballsed up your last three jobs.'

'Yeah? Who nicked the dip we'd been chasing for weeks?'

'From what I hear, young Leo.'

'You believe in fairies?'

'Only the kind without wings.'

'It'll be a long time before he's up to nicking a blind beggar.' Myers turned and spoke to Kendrick. 'I suppose all you've been doing except talking balls is waiting to be told what to do?'

'I phoned the hospital to find out how Mrs Lynch is.'

'If you're not careful, you'll be showing some initiative. How is she?'

'She's had an operation for a broken femur and bad bruising and is recovering in intensive care. Another thing, the lab phoned earlier; I've put a note of their report on your desk.'

Myers looked down at the muddle of files and books, picked up a single sheet of paper, and read. 'Not telling us anything fresh. Penfold was so pissed, he saw five old women and never knew which was the one he hit.'

'Which seems funny.'

'An old biddy gets knocked down and half-killed and that makes you laugh?'

'Funny peculiar. If he was that tight, how come he could drive at all? Yet he managed to get from Oak Cross to home without ending up in a ditch or wrapped around a tree.'

'Drunken luck. Where's the report from Vehicles?'

'I haven't been on to them yet because . . .'

'Because that's asking too much from you.'

Kendrick phoned Vehicles at county HQ. An ill-tempered sergeant said that if they had checked the Jaguar and found something to report, it would have been reported; but they had not even started on it because there were a dozen other vehicles that had to be examined first, yet hadn't been because there was always some silly sod interrupting their work with useless questions.

He replaced the receiver. 'They've not yet got around to examining the Jaguar.'

'Why not?'

'Pressure of work.'

'That's what they claim? A right bunch of comics!'

In his present mood, Kendrick decided, Myers would accuse a choir of angels of singing out of tune.

Six

The weak sunlight formed a right angle of shadow in the centre of the sitting room and almost reached the open fireplace that backed the one in the priest's room, both of which had been built when the open hall, which had reached up to the roof, had been divided to provide considerably more accommodation.

'Is there anything you'd like?' Lucy asked.

'Only a new head and stomach,' Penfold answered.

'Things aren't settling down?'

'They're possibly settling, but are a long way from settled. The mother of all hangovers without the pleasure of having enjoyed the drinking: a definition of injustice.' He stared through the single window at the lawn and the carefully clipped yew hedge that marked the end of the garden and beyond which the tops of trees in the orchard were visible. 'Do you think . . . Will the police believe me?'

'Of course they will, since you'll be telling them the simple truth.'

'"The truth is rarely pure, and never simple." So will they have sufficient imagination to accept complication? . . . The first thing, as you said, is that they're going to look for an explanation of what happened.'

'What are you going to say?'

'Perhaps they mistook me for someone else.'

'When they obviously knew where you lived?'

'They could have found the address from the papers in the car.'

'Yes, of course. I'm sorry.'

'For what?'

'For maybe sounding as if . . .'

'. . . you still didn't believe me? I know you do, but it's no good forgetting you found that difficult to begin with. And if you did, won't the police find it infinitely more so?'

'They'll work things out. And the reason will turn out to be like a crossword clue.'

'How's that?'

'It'll make sense when one knows the answer.'

'If the puzzle was set by Torquemada, it still won't . . . I'm rather surprised the police haven't turned up yet.'

'I'm sure that's a good sign. They know you told them the truth and are reluctant to come and apologize for last night – if that nasty little man is capable of apologizing.'

'He was that rude?'

'Not so much in words, but in manner. I got the impression he was being as objectionable as he dared; it was almost as if he was enjoying seeing me so distressed . . . But I expect that's all imagination . . . You haven't forgotten tomorrow, have you?'

'Something significant is happening?'

'You *had* forgotten! But in the circumstances, I'll forgive you. It's Founder's Day at Ransley Hall, and after the thanksgiving service everyone's free until six in the evening, so we're taking Charles out to lunch.'

Lucy's one regret concerning their marriage – as far as he knew – was that she had been denied the pigeon pair of children she had always wanted. Charles was in his third year at prep school. 'I'm likely to be lousy company, so maybe you should go on your own?'

'By then, everything will have been cleared up, so we're both going. I said we'd pick him up at eleven thirty, which is when they come out of chapel. He's decided we'll eat at Chez Pauline.'

'The best is just good enough?'

'He's certain their chocolate mousse was composed in heaven. And you'd have been most disappointed had he chosen hamburgers and fries.'

'Would I?'

'You know how old-fashioned you can be. It's not long ago that Charles asked me if you'd been born when Queen Victoria was on the throne.'

'The expensive education he's receiving is obviously a waste of money.'

She smiled. 'I sometimes think most conventional education is a waste of time and money, but it's nice to maintain tradition, since so much is disappearing in the name of a modern world.'

'What tradition? I didn't go to Ransley Hall.'

'But both my father and grandfather did, and if you're trying to make out there's only paternally inspired tradition, you're being a real male chauvinist.'

'A man has to maintain his position in days of rampant feminism . . . I hope that what's happened to me won't have any effect on him.'

'Of course it won't.'

Detective Inspector Ingham walked a straight path through life. Right was right, wrong was wrong, and it was sophistry to try to argue that the one could sometimes meld into the other; rules had to be obeyed and if their observance resulted in unfortunate consequences, it was the rules, not the administration of them, which were at fault. No man could have a more worthy ambition than to do his duty at all times. His superiors marked him an excellent officer, his juniors sometimes referred to him as Dinosaur.

He looked across his desk at Detective Sergeant Clemens. 'Do we have a preliminary report from the lab on the thread from the headlamp?'

'Vehicles haven't yet sent it on; they say that's because they're short-staffed and overburdened with work.'

'Are they ever anything else?'

Clemens wasn't certain whether or not that was a question tinged with sardonic humour. He could hardly have been of a more different nature from Ingham. If he had had a philosophy of life, it would have held that since people died from overwork, the sensible man took great care not to suffer such stress.

'Can we continue to hold the car without the specific authority if he's not charged or under arrest?'

'I think we should be OK claiming further examination has to be carried out for his benefit as well as ours.'

'You only think?'

If that was meant to criticize him for not being certain, Clemens thought resentfully, the DI might remember that he didn't seem to know for certain either.

Ingham looked at his watch. 'I can't go on waiting for Vehicles to pull their fingers out . . . I've told Myers I want him along. So see he's standing by for a midday take-off to question Penfold.' Most DIs often referred to their DCs by their christian names; Ingham seldom did. 'And Kendrick had better be with us . . . How's he making out?'

'Dave says he's sharp enough, but too ready to jump to imaginative conclusions.'

'Damning with faint criticism?'

Clemens failed to appreciate the misquote.

'I have wondered whether Myers was the right man for him to work with.'

'Dave knows the job backwards.'

'A pedant would comment that it would be better to be forward-looking . . . All right, that's it.' Clemens, his figure sufficiently rotund occasionally to provoke sarcastic mirth, left.

The DI liked driving, but his passengers seldom enjoyed being driven by him: he had an acutely accurate judgement

41

of distance that often led them to believe their last moments had arrived.

'It's the next place on the right,' Myers said from the front passenger seat. He was grateful the journey was about to end.

The DI slowed, turned into the drive, braked to a stop. 'Nice to own a house like this,' he said, his hands still on the wheel as he stared through the windscreen at Alten Cobb. 'What would you say – seventeenth century?'

'Could be,' Myers answered, in the tone of someone who couldn't tell seventeenth-century architecture from nineteenth and didn't regret this deficiency.

'I think it's mainly early fifteenth, sir,' Kendrick said.

'What makes you say that?'

'I read an article about the place.'

'You're interested in old houses?'

'Not so much in the house as its history. Alten Cobb was owned by the same family until they backed the wrong side in the Civil War. One of the Tores, who lived there previously, is supposed to have given sanctuary to a priest who was later captured and executed, but historians argue as to whether that's fact.'

'Historians will argue about yesterday. It's good to hear someone's interested in local history.'

Myers said, 'For my money, give me a modern house that isn't about to fall down because of dry rot, wet rot, and Colorado beetle.'

'Death-watch beetle,' Ingham corrected.

Myers silently swore.

Ingham climbed out of the car, led the way to the gate and stepped into the garden. As Kendrick followed the other two around the house to the front door, he mused on the fact that appearances really were often deceptive. An historically old house in near-perfect condition, a lawn that resembled a bowling green and flower beds that still managed to provide colour seemed to approach as near to Shangri-La as mortal

42

man was allowed, yet the Penfolds must be experiencing fear, not composed pleasure.

Ingham banged twice on the wooden door with the heavy wrought-iron knocker in the form of a fox's head. The door was opened.

'Mr Penfold?'

'Yes.'

'Detective Inspector Ingham, DC Myers and PC Kendrick, both of whom were here last night.' As he spoke, he produced his warrant card and opened it out. 'I should like to ask some questions, so may we come in?' He replaced it in his pocket. As he stepped inside and looked around himself, he said, 'You have a very lovely house.'

'We like it,' Penfold replied shortly. And then, accepting the stupidity of appearing to be rude, he added, 'We were very lucky it was for sale when we were looking for a house . . . Would you like to come through?'

He led the way into the priest's room. Lucy sat beyond the fireplace, in which a small fire burned for the visual pleasure only since radiators kept the room warm.

'Detective Inspector Ingham,' Penfold said to Lucy. 'And I think you've met—'

'Yes,' she said, interrupting him.

The previous night Myers must have said or done something – probably both – to annoy her, Ingham judged. Not that that would have been difficult. There was character in her face; when her family was threatened, she would fight.

'Do please sit,' she said formally.

Ingham settled on one of the armchairs that ringed the fireplace. 'Mr Penfold, I think you know that last night at around seven thirty, in Oak Cross, an elderly woman was knocked down by a car which did not stop.'

'Yes,' he answered, aware his voice had sharpened from tension.

'An eyewitness managed to read most of the registration

number of the car and to identify its make; because of this, DC Myers and PC Kendrick came here to ask you to help in their enquiries.'

She said, 'Your officer had a strange way of asking for help. I'd describe his manner as accusatory rather than supplicatory.'

'All I—' Myers began.

Ingham cut his words short. 'I'm sorry if that's how it seemed, Mrs Penfold, but there are times when circumstances don't allow us to be quite as polite as we would wish . . . And perhaps I might now ask you one or two questions politely?' He smiled.

Her expression remained taut.

'Do you know what the time was when your husband returned last night?'

'No.'

'How did he get here?'

'In his car.'

'His Jaguar?'

'Yes.'

'How would you describe his physical condition when he arrived here?'

'Terrible.'

'Would you like to be a little more precise?'

'He'd been disgustingly sick over himself and the car and had so little control over his legs I had a terrible job to get him into the house.'

'Had you any idea what he was suffering from?'

'He was drunk.'

Ingham could not hide his astonishment at the blunt answer. 'You thought he had been drinking heavily?'

'As I have just said. Naturally, when they came here . . .' She looked briefly at Myers. 'I tried to make out he was suffering from some illness.'

'Why was that?'

'Surely that's obvious,' Penfold said. 'She wanted to

conceal the fact that I was drunk, believing I had been driving my car.'

'And you hadn't?'

'No.'

'Then who drove it from Oak Cross to here?'

'I've no idea.'

'I'm afraid I don't understand what you're telling me.'

'When I left the office—'

'At what time?'

'Just after seven. I heard the church clock strike, realized it was considerably later than I'd thought and hurried down to my car.'

'Had you been drinking alcohol in your office?'

'No.'

'Did you stop at a pub on your way home?'

'No.'

'Then how do you explain that you were drunk by the time you arrived here?'

'I saw a Saab coming up from Weedenhurst, but because it would meet the 'Stop' sign, I carried on. It didn't stop, but came out in front of me, forcing me to brake very fiercely. Another car drove up behind me and boxed me in and they forced me to stop. When men got out, faces covered in ski-masks, I was certain they were going to rob me and take the car, but they grabbed me, gagged me, pulled a ski-mask over my face, secured my wrists and ankles, shoved me into the back well of my car, and then three of them got into it and drove off. The driver thought he was Formula One material. We went round a corner at God-knows-what speed, there was a bump and someone shouted we'd hit her. Another of them used a mobile to report what had happened and then said to drive to an all-night supermarket and buy a litre bottle of whisky. There was an argument about this, but that didn't last and we stopped and one of them bought the bottle.

'We drove for a time, stopped again; they dragged me out of the car, rolled up the ski-mask above my mouth and

Jeffrey Ashford

forced me to swallow the whisky. Somewhat naturally, I don't remember much more.'

'You didn't meet Father Christmas?' Myers asked.

'Enough of that!' Ingham snapped.

'It's the truth,' Lucy said angrily.

'Then why didn't you inform the officers of this last night?'

'How was I to know what had happened before Gavin was able to tell me?'

'Then you didn't actually see the Jaguar arrive back or the men who'd been in it?'

'No,' she finally said.

'Was there another car in your drive or leaving it?'

'No.'

'Did you hear a car drive away?'

'No. But I was too worried to notice anything. Gavin's promised me that it's the truth, so I know it is . . . You do believe that, don't you?'

'It's far too early in the investigation to make any definite judgement.'

'Your tone of voice says what you think.'

'Then I apologize for my tone.'

'That's right, laugh at me.'

'Mrs Penfold, I am certainly not laughing at you.'

'Did you hear Gavin tell you they bought a bottle of whisky at the supermarket?'

'Of course.'

'He does not like whisky and never drinks it.'

Ingham spoke to Penfold. 'That is fact?'

'I've just told you,' she said angrily.

'I never drink it,' Penfold said. Then he added, 'Willingly.'

'You have a cellar?'

'There's one that was built out from the side of the house by a previous owner.'

'Do you keep whisky in it?'

'Naturally, but it's for offering to friends, not for me. I

46

repeat; I never choose to drink whisky . . . I know what I've told you sounds crazy, but it's what happened.'

'Why should anyone wish to kidnap you?'

'Maybe they didn't; maybe they mistook me for some-one else.'

'If so, I'd expect them to abandon you when they discov-ered their mistake rather than bring you back here.'

'Then it was because of my job.'

'Which is what?'

'Network architect, specializing in security, with the Counties Bank.'

'That must be a very responsible position?'

'It is.'

'Demanding a person of irreproachable character?'

'Yes.'

'So were it ever shown you had driven your car when drunk, knocked down a woman and injured her severely, then continued without stopping to call for help, your employers might well think you no longer fit to hold that position?'

'I don't know how they'd regard an incident that had nothing to do with the job or my ability to carry that out conscientiously.'

'But I imagine you probably could judge . . . Can you describe the men who attacked you?'

'No.'

'You noticed nothing about them as they left their cars and approached yours?'

'They'd ski-masks over their faces and took care to keep out of the headlights. In any case, I was too confused – scared – to try to note anything. And as I've already said, as soon as they got hold of me, they pulled what I think was a ski-mask back-to-front over my head so that I couldn't see anything.'

'You can't say whether any of them was noticeably tall, short, thin or fat?'

47

'I wasn't conscious of anything but the need to try to save myself.'

'Did you hear them speak?'

'Yes.'

'How would you describe their voices?'

'Rough, uneducated.'

'Obviously not from good families,' Myers said sarcastically.

'Thank you,' Ingham said, meaning 'Shut up'. 'Were any names mentioned, Mr Penfold?'

'Al was the driver of the Jaguar. The two other men were Bert and Ed. When one of them was talking over a mobile to someone who was giving the orders, that person's name was Reg.'

'Did they tell you where they were driving you?'

'No.'

'After leaving the supermarket, they stopped somewhere and forced you to drink the whole of the bottle of whisky before driving here. Can you say where that stop was made?'

'Not for certain, no.'

'What precisely does that mean?'

'They dragged me out of the car and rolled up the mask only until it was clear of my mouth, so I still couldn't see. But traffic was passing and seemed to be running parallel to where I was, so perhaps it was a lay-by.'

'You had become more observant than before?'

'Does that make me a liar?'

'Of course not. After you had been forced to drink the whisky, did they drive straight here?'

'God knows! My head and stomach were going round in circles.'

'And when the car arrived here, what happened?'

'All I can remember is being dragged out of the back well, having the mask and tape removed, and being shoved behind the wheel.'

'Presumably there was another car in which the men left?'

'I don't know.'

'You didn't hear a car drive off?'

'No.'

'Is there anything more you can tell us?'

'No.'

'Then that about covers all the questions we need to ask for the moment.' Ingham stood. Myers and Kendrick, after they'd pocketed their notebooks, did the same. 'Thank you for your help.'

Lucy spoke vehemently. 'You're so certain Gavin's lying, you haven't listened to a word he's said.'

'Mrs Penfold,' Ingham answered, 'I assure you I have noted everything, and full enquiries will be made to substantiate your husband's story.'

'His "story". That just shows what you really think.'

'We often refer to a witness's statement as his story. It carries no derogatory inference.'

'Doesn't it? . . . You must understand, he's telling the truth.'

'Then you may rest assured that we should be able to confirm it. Please don't bother to see us out.' Ingham, followed by Myers and Kendrick, left.

Lucy and Penfold did not speak for quite a while.

Seven

'What's the verdict?' Ingham asked, as he drove out on to the road and skilfully avoided an oncoming car that was travelling in the middle of the lane.

'Never heard such a load of balls.' Myers spoke more bluntly than intended, but he was nervously certain a collision had been missed by no more than an inch.

'It's an intriguing story.'

'He must think we're plods if he expects us to swallow it.'

'Then what's your interpretation of events?'

'Maybe started boozing in town, stopped off to empty the bottle of whisky in the car, was so pissed he never saw Muriel Lynch until he hit her, realized he had to clear off as quickly as possible in the hopes no one had been able to identify the car.'

'So where do we go from here?'

'Wait for forensic to supply the evidence, then charge him.'

'You dismiss out of hand what he says?'

'When you told her it was a story, I reckon that was a hundred and one per cent correct.'

'A judgement which you made rather obvious.'

'Sir,' Myers said, resentful at having been rebuked in front of Kendrick.

Ingham was silent for a moment, then said, 'So what's your assessment of his evidence?'

Kendrick correctly assumed it was he who was being asked. 'On the face of things, it does sound absurd, sir.'

'But?'

'He must realize it does, so if he were lying, wouldn't he offer a more believable story?'

'If villains were sharp, we wouldn't ever nick 'em,' Myers muttered.

Ingham said, 'Because we can never be quite as sharp?'

'I wasn't . . . All I was trying to say, Guv, is that it's ten to one he'd been on the booze and is now offering a ridiculous story in the hopes we're soft enough to swallow it because he is who he is.'

'Isn't the question, in part, who is he?' Ingham braked to a halt at a crossroads, then drew across in the face of an oncoming car – a perfectly safe manoeuvre, but one that had Myers once more bracing himself for the crash. 'So what next?'

'Like I said.'

'Kendrick?'

'Sir, I think we should look for evidence that would back up his story.'

'And waste time and effort when we can't even keep up with things that matter?' Myers muttered.

'You wouldn't agree with the dictum that our job should be as concerned with proving innocence as guilt?' Ingham asked. 'He's a security expert with a very large bank, so if he is telling the truth, the motive for the night's happenings must surely be connected with that fact.'

'If.'

'We'll find out at the bank if anyone can verify that Penfold left just after seven, as he claims, and whether he appeared sober. If he did, then since the accident was at seven thirty-five, there's hardly the time for him to have become so thoroughly drunk.'

'What's to say he was pissed to the gills by the time of the accident?' Myers asked. 'A couple of doubles in a pub don't take long and that could be enough alcohol to have him driving dangerously. After he'd hit her, he tried to drink the

51

memory away with the bottle he kept in the car or had bought at a pub.'

'So question bartenders at the pubs that lie along his route home.'

'That'll take a long time.'

'Only if the questioner doesn't have a dry throat . . . Find out if we can determine whether the bottle of whisky was bought in a supermarket.'

'Sir, we're short-handed . . .'

'Was there a cap on the whisky bottle found in the Jaguar?'

There was a silence.

'Obviously, elementary observations were not made, probably because of the certainty that the improbable was impossible.'

Another silence.

They came in sight of the large, graceless building, once a remand home for youngsters, that marked the outskirts of Pettersgrove.

'Penfold reckons he was in a lay-by when forced to drink the whisky. Assuming the direct route from Pettersgrove was taken, that suggests the one on the main road beyond Firfield, doesn't it?'

'Yes, sir,' Myers answered.

'Search there for anything that might back up his story.'

Penfold stared through the single window of the breakfast room at the lawn, flower bed, yew hedge and distant woods. Nothing was more beautiful than when its loss seemed possible. 'How the hell do I begin to make them believe me?'

'I think . . .' Lucy began, then stopped.

'What?'

'I'm sure the detective inspector was more open-minded than Myers, who obviously would have liked to arrest you then and there.'

He looked back and at her. 'But how open-minded does

he have to be to accept I'm telling the truth? I'd have to be a fool not to appreciate how crazy it all sounds. So crazy, I'm contradicting myself. One moment I'm complaining they won't believe me, the next admitting how difficult, perhaps impossible, that is.'

'I'm sure it would help if you could suggest why those men kidnapped you.'

'The only suggestion I can come up with is that the reason has to be connected with my job.'

'But in what way?'

'I don't know. I don't bloody know.'

'Gavin, I'm only trying to help.'

'Yes, but it's like being strapped down, legs apart, and hearing the circular saw pass between my feet . . . Presumably, they hoped to force me to help them defraud the bank.'

'How?'

'In any one of dozens of possible ways. Obviously, running into that woman ruined their plans.' He walked over to one of the armchairs, sat. 'The police are close to arresting me.'

'Gavin, that's nonsense!'

'No, it isn't. If they do arrest me, what will people think? What will your parents think?'

'That the police are stupid.'

'At first, maybe. But when the facts come out, won't people begin to wonder . . .'

'Stop talking like that. You're innocent.'

'Innocence can become a very weak defence when compared to the imagination of a good lie. If I can't prove I was not driving the Jag when it hit the woman – and how often can one prove a negative? – I am going to be arrested.'

'The truth always comes out.'

'Only in never-never land . . . I remember your mother telling me that all she and your father asked of me was that I made you happy.'

'Which you have – always.'

Jeffrey Ashford

'But if I'm branded a drunken driver who ran down a woman and didn't stop to help her because I didn't even know what I'd done, you're going to become very unhappy. Your parents will blame me.'

'I'll make them understand you've told the truth. They'll do anything they can to help you. Why are you talking like this?'

'Because there are times when one has to face the future. There's bound to be a corner in their minds, because of the past, in which there'll be questions such as: Did I forget my promise to you to curb my drinking?'

'No. No. No. What's got into you?'

'A bottle of whisky that made me first ill and then terrified our lives are going to be wrenched apart.'

She stood, crossed to his chair, put her arms around him and drew his head against herself. 'Whatever happens, my darling, our lives are joined together, and the only thing that can separate them is the death of one of us; and if there really is a God, that separation won't be for long.'

As he drove into the lay-by, Kendrick was satisfied he'd been left to make the search on his own because Myers was not only lazy but convinced it would be a total waste of time. It was angled at its centre point and was separated from the present road by a screen of trees and undergrowth, much of it brambles.

He parked behind a Ford in which a couple were enjoying each other's company. They reminded him of two nights ago when Margaret and he had parked off-road on top of Devil's Dyke. Soon afterwards, perhaps remembering her mother's suspicious advice, she had said they must stop, since someone might see them. His plea that that could only be if the someone had night-vision glasses had not been well received.

He used the stick he'd brought to part the grass, weeds and brambles in his search. Myers had told him to report immediately if he found a pumpkin and four white mice so

54

that they could both get to the ball on time; Myers's humour was always leaden. All that he did find for a while was evidence that this was a favourite spot for couples; then, near the exit, he saw a cream-coloured bottle top on which was printed an invitation to visit the Famous Grouse experience and the details of a web site.

He used a handkerchief to pick up the cap, dropped it into a small plastic exhibit bag and recorded on the label the location, time and date. The Investigation Handbook (the CID recruit's bible) laid it down that no search could be considered completed unless and until the searcher could be certain there was nothing more to be found. (How could one be certain unless one knew what was there to be found? If one knew, why was one having to search to find out?) He returned to the exit and began again. When he was level with the Ford, the back nearside window was wound down sufficiently for a sweaty red-headed man belligerently to threaten to rend him limb from limb if he went on peeping. When he identified himself, the window was hastily closed, a partially clad man scrambled over the front seat, and the car drove off.

Later, having found nothing more during the second search, he settled behind the wheel of the CID car, but did not immediately start the engine. The other man had been convinced he was a peeping Tom. Why? Because he had passed the car thrice and each time had instinctively looked at it, as any policeman would. He knew he had not been peeping, but the couple inside the car would never believe that. Circumstances could fictionalize the truth.

Myers stared down at the plastic bag, containing the bottle top, on his desk.

'That bears out what he told us,' Kendrick said. 'The bottle was opened, he heard the cap thrown away into the undergrowth, they made him drink. The bottle in the car was the Famous Grouse so it would have to be an extraordinary coincidence if this cap didn't come from that bottle.'

'If you'd served long enough to learn anything, you'd know that coincidences are two a penny.'

'The top is so clean, it can't have been there for any length of time.'

'You know what kind of metal it's made of?'

'No.'

'Or what effect weather will have on it?'

'No.'

'Then leave it to someone who does to say how long it's been there.'

'So I take it along to the guv'nor now?'

'And don't hand him any of your opinions because he's no time for stupidity.'

Kendrick picked up the bag, left the room and went along the passage; the door of the DI's office was partially open, so he knocked and entered. Ingham, seated behind the desk and working at papers, looked up.

'I'm just back from searching the lay-by, sir.' Kendrick put the bag on the desk. 'I found this.'

Ingham picked up the bag and visually examined the cap through the transparent plastic, then put the bag down. 'Where exactly was it?'

'Fifteen feet from the exit and three feet into the undergrowth.'

'Get it off to the lab and ask them to tell us anything they can.' He leaned back in his chair. 'Does it say anything to you?'

'I reckon it backs up Mr Penfold's story.'

'Why?'

'He said the men opened the whisky bottle in the lay-by. It would be the natural thing to throw the cap away, knowing the bottle was going to be emptied. Both cap and bottle are of the same brand.'

'If Penfold's story is true, would the villains not be trying their best to make certain there was no evidence to support him?'

'They probably thought we'd be so ready to disbelieve him, we'd never check the lay-by. Or they were just careless.'

'I've just pointed out that, logically, they would have taken care not to be careless.'

'Yes, sir. But sometimes tension upsets logic. And like as not, whoever threw it away didn't think it could ever mean much.'

'He could be right; it'll need the lab to tell us whether it's possible to say the cap came from the bottle in the car.'

'I'm certain it did.'

'You need to remember the best advice I was ever given: fit a theory to the facts, not the facts to a theory.'

'It's just . . .'

'Well?'

'Something recently happened that made me realize how easily one can come to totally the wrong conclusion because of a faulty interpretation of the facts.'

'Then you've learned something valuable . . . Has Myers told you what to do next?'

'No, sir.'

'In the light of Penfold's evidence, there are only two all-night supermarkets at which the whisky could have been bought. See the managements and find out if there's any way in which they can confirm the sale of a single litre bottle of Famous Grouse on Friday night between nineteen thirty-five and twenty thirty. They'll try to say that's impossible, so explain how important the information is.'

Back in the CID general room, Bonner was sitting on the corner of Myers's desk, talking to him. Myers, clearly bored, interrupted the self-congratulatory story to call out, 'What did the guv'nor say?'

'Send it to the lab,' Kendrick answered.

'Send what?' Bonner asked.

'A bottle top that probably came off the bottle found in Penfold's car.'

'But more likely didn't,' Myers said. 'Why are we wasting

time? Penfold got pissed, knocked the woman down, and is now trying to feed us a cock-and-bull story because his kind reckons they can do what they want and never be held to account.'

'So what's his kind?' Bonner asked as he slid off the desk.

'An army of ancestors.'

'And you're envious because you haven't any?'

'You know what I bloody mean.' Myers turned to Kendrick. 'If you've been told to get the cap to the lab, what's the point of standing there?'

'I was waiting for the chance to tell you I'm off to the supermarkets to see if one of 'em recorded a sale of a single litre bottle of the Famous Grouse.'

'They'll laugh in your face. I'm not having you waste any more time, so you can forget that and file this load of bumf.' He tapped a small pile of memoranda from county HQ.

'If filing that lot isn't a waste of time, what the hell is?' Bonner asked.

'Dave, it was the guv'nor who said to talk to the super-markets.'

'Then he's going soft, thinking the story could begin to be true.'

'Won't he be making as certain as possible that no smart mouthpiece can fool the jury in Penfold's favour?' Bonner suggested.

'I suppose there's something in that,' Myers admitted reluctantly.

'Right, I'm off. And as I'm not on Sunday duty, I won't see you until Monday, bright-eyed and bushy-tailed.'

'Red-eyed and broken-tailed more likely.'

Bonner laughed. 'Jealousy will get you nowhere.' He left.

Myers said aggressively, 'D'you intend to stand there for the rest of the day instead of wasting your time asking supermarkets sodding stupid questions?'

Kendrick followed Bonner out of the room.

There were two twenty-four-hour supermarkets in Pettersgrove, one to the north and the other to the south of the town. Muriel Lynch had been knocked down in Oak Cross, so logically, had the car turned back to buy whisky, it would have driven to the one to the south.

Kendrick switched off the engine, checked the time: half past six. He was due at Margaret's house at seven for supper. Her mother, old-fashioned in too many ways, strongly disliked bad time-keeping. Let him be at all late and the evening would become frosty. There were moments when he wondered how closely a daughter might grow to resemble her mother.

One of the stackers in the supermarket, hard at work since there were relatively few customers, directed him to the office, which lay beyond the stores area. He walked past blocks of cartons to the small complex of two rooms, in the first of which a woman, nearing middle age, worked at a computer. She told him Mr Harold had left, but the assistant manager was next door and she'd find out if he was free. After a quick word through the open doorway, she told him to go through.

Betts was a harassed man. 'I hope there's no trouble?'

He would always wish trouble on to someone else's shoulders, Kendrick thought. 'Nothing to cause concern. I'm here just to ask if you'll do something for us.'

'Of course.' Relief gave way to caution. 'That is, if I can . . . Do sit.'

Kendrick sat. 'We're conducting an important investigation and need to know if someone came into this store and bought just a litre bottle of Famous Grouse whisky, nothing more.'

'You what?' Amazement caused Betts's voice to rise. 'Don't you know we sell heaven-knows-how-many bottles of that brand . . .'

'It's not an open-ended problem. I can give the date and

the time within maybe an hour, and like I said, that's all the purchaser bought. Till and maybe automatic stock records could pick out the purchase, couldn't they?'

Betts nervously tapped his fingers on the desk. 'I suppose it might just be possible to identify such a purchase, but even so, unless the customer used a card, there's no way of knowing who he was.'

'That would be a bonus, but the important thing right now is to learn if there was such a purchase.'

'You're saying you're not even certain there was?'

'Put it this way: we need to confirm what we believe.'

'I don't understand.'

'Please just go along with things – the information really is important.'

'Well . . . There's a problem.'

'Which is?'

'I'd have to put someone on to checking records, which would mean work wouldn't get done on time. Management is very critical when that sort of thing happens, and it's difficult to make them understand.'

'If they start bitching, point out how it pays to co-operate with us, because then we'll always be in a rush to help you if there's trouble.' He gave the relevant date and times, making it obvious he assumed his request would be met; he thanked Betts for the 'willing' help and left.

Eight

When on Sunday duty, Myers provided even greyer company than usual. A natural pessimism increased and old resentments were aired yet again, often with added prejudices. As Kendrick listened to a lecture on the evils of wealth, he wondered why Myers bought three lottery tickets each week – in order to gain personal experience of those evils?

Ingham entered the room. 'Any result from the super-markets?'

'No, sir,' Kendrick replied. 'Both said it would take time to go through the records and in any case probably they wouldn't be able to tell us anything.'

'The standard ploy of their ilk. If you don't hear very soon, chivvy them up . . . Penfold says he left the office at seven, Friday evening. If that can be confirmed, his story gets some solid backing because of the time elements.'

'Not if he was half-cut when he left it,' Myers said.

'Unlikely. No bank's going to employ as their IT expert someone who drinks during working hours . . . Is anyone else in now?'

'No, sir, on account of Young having been on a course . . .'

'Then Kendrick can question the guard.' He spoke to Kendrick. 'Find out if there were any signs of Penfold's having been drinking that evening. If the guard's reluctant to say anything because of a false sense of loyalty, remind him the victim was an old woman, severely injured. Has someone been on to the hospital this morning to find out how she is?'

There was no answer.

'Sunday offers no excuses for slackness.' He left.

'That bloody man is causing nothing but trouble,' Myers said resentfully.

'Isn't that half the job of a DI?'

'Penfold, not the guv'nor. Resentful just because we dare ask him questions.'

'If he's telling the truth, I'd say he's got a right to feel resentful at the way some people respond.'

'You're so naive, you probably believe there are toms with hearts of gold.'

'There must be some who'd respond if life would let 'em.'

'Yeah, respond by kicking the punters in the nuts . . . When Penfold's kind is in trouble, there's no room for the truth. He'd lie at the Pearly Gates if that would get him inside.'

'How could it, when his lies would be recognized immediately?'

'You're an expert on security in heaven?'

'Not exactly.'

'Then belt up.'

'I reckon he could be telling the truth.'

'Then how about putting your money where your mouth is? Fifty quid he gets sent down.'

'Bet on his being convicted?'

'Not so certain now, are you?'

'I'm certain we'd be dead stupid to make that sort of a bet.'

'No bottle, that's you.'

'What d'you think the guv'nor would have to say if he heard about it?'

'That if you're backing Penfold to escape being sent down, you'd follow a three-legged horse in the Grand National.'

Kendrick picked up his notebook, stood.

'Where d'you think you're going?'

'To talk to whichever guard was on duty at the bank on Friday night.'

'Why?'

'You heard the guv'nor.'

'Forget that. There's cross-checking to do in the hardware job.'

'So when he asks me what the guard said, I explain I don't know because you countermanded his orders?'

'If he said walk, you'd run to try to make yourself look good,' was Myers's sour comment.

Twenty minutes later, Kendrick parked on the solid line outside the glass-and-concrete building which, the architect claimed, captured the powerful freedom of a square-rigger under full sail – to the average person, its maritime resemblance was to a waterlogged hulk.

There was a small courtyard, the entrance to which was guarded by a barrier. He pressed the entry call button and identified himself. The barrier lifted. He passed a stone fountain in which half a dozen koi carp led a lazy life, reached ten-foot-high glass entrance doors. Immediately inside, a uniformed guard waited. He opened his warrant card and held it up against the glass; the guard activated the locking mechanism, opened the right-hand door. The atrium was almost large enough to house the architect's square-rigger.

'So what's the problem?' the guard asked.

'I want a chat with whoever was on duty Friday evening.'

'That'll be George – he's on nights.'

'Can you give me his address?'

'Not out of me head, but I can look it up. In a spot of bother, is he?'

'No.'

'Just want a chat with him about the weather?' The guard smirked. 'If you ask me, the next thing I'll hear about him is he's spending the rest of his life on his yacht in Bermuda.'

Five minutes later, Kendrick left the building; sixteen minutes after that, he braked to a halt outside Seacrest

House, a block of twelve flats on the north-east side of the town.

The front door of 11c was opened by a woman who had an apron over her dress. He introduced himself.

'What's up, then?'

Since the average person's reaction to learning his professional identity was sudden concern, it seemed the average person had a guilty conscience. 'Nothing to worry about, Mrs Cameron. I'd just like a word with your husband.'

'But he's in bed. Works nights.'

'I'm sorry to turn up like this, but I do need to talk to him urgently.'

'Then I suppose you'd best come in.'

He stepped into a narrow area that was more passage than hall in which there was the scent of roasting meat. 'Smells like there's a tasty meal coming up.' (Operational Manual: 'Always try to promote a friendly atmosphere by admiring something; babies can be the most rewarding subjects.')

'George likes a nice bit of roast when he gets up on Sunday morning. Really goes for his lamb . . .'

He listened to an account of Cameron's eating habits as he followed her into the sitting room.

'Sorry about the state,' she said, 'only there's not been the time to clear up.' She moved a rumpled newspaper off a chair and picked up a small ball of wool from the floor. 'I'll tell him,' she said, as she put the newspaper and wool on the coffee table, picked up two dirty mugs and carried these out of the room.

The minutes passed. He tried to remember how long Rip Van Winkle had slept? . . .

Cameron finally entered, a heavily built man in his late thirties; untidy hair and an unshaven face testified to his unwelcome awakening. 'She says you want a word?' He slumped down on the nearest chair.

'That's right. Sorry to have disturbed you . . .'

'Not half as sorry as me.'

Kendrick smiled.

'So what's it about?'

'We're making certain enquiries and think you may be able to help us.'

'Like how?'

'First, can you confirm you were on night duty at the bank on Friday?'

'Yeah.'

'What are your hours?'

'Six to six.'

'You're always on nights?'

'Prefer it. 'Cept when I'm woken up early.'

'I'll be as quick as possible so you can get back to sleep.'

'Ain't possible after I get woke.'

There was no helping some people. 'Tell me about the security at the bank.'

The control desk was in full view of the main entrance and from there were controlled CCTV cameras, alarm indicators, and a panic button connected directly to the nearest police station. Emergency fire exits had one-way doors, which were wired to alarms and under the surveillance of cameras – staff were specifically forbidden to use such exits except in an emergency.

'So when you're on duty, you see everyone who leaves or enters the building?'

'That's right.'

'When do most of the staff finish work?'

'Five.'

'Do many remain after then?'

'Quite often there's one or two working late.'

'And you'd see each such person leave?'

'Unless I was making a round.'

'Did you make a round last Friday at seven in the evening?'

'Not as I remember, but I can't say for certain without checking the log.'

'What's that?'

Cameron became loquacious. As far as the guards were concerned, security at the bank was tight enough to make a man look in a mirror and be suspicious of whom he was seeing. Every time one left the control desk, one had to note the fact in the log – even if just making tea or having a Jimmy Riddle – and at the end of each round, had to confirm in writing that all doors and windows had been checked, CCTV cameras and monitors tested and found active . . .

'I suppose the guard I spoke to at Hallam House earlier will be there on duty?'

'If he ain't, he'll be shot.'

'Would you ring and ask him to check the log book to find out whether you were making a round between seven and seven-thirty on Friday?'

'Here, what's this all about?'

'I need to know if and when you saw someone leaving the building.'

'Who?'

'Let's leave that until we know for sure you were at the control desk between those two times.'

He hesitated and seemed to be about to ask more questions, then heaved himself up and left. When he returned, he said, 'I made me first round at ten past six and the next at nine.'

'How long does a round take?'

'Twenty minutes, if there ain't no bother.'

'Then you were back at the desk by six thirty?'

'Yeah.'

'Is there any record of you leaving the desk between the two rounds?'

'Can't be.'

'Why not?'

'Ain't allowed to make tea until after the nine o'clock round.'

Cameron, Kendrick noted, had begun to speak defensively. 'And you didn't visit the toilet?'

'The log says as I didn't move until the nine o'clock round.'

'Were any of the staff working late that night?'

'I recollect a couple left after the rest.'

'Can you identify them?'

'One was Wraith; the other was the red-head secretary – can't give her a name.'

'No one else?'

'No.'

'You know Mr Penfold?'

'Yes.'

'You didn't see him leave the building very soon after seven?'

'No.'

'You can be quite certain of that?'

'Ain't I just said?'

'You couldn't have left the desk and just forgotten to note the fact in the log as it was only for so short a time?'

'If I leave, I write, like the rules say.' Cameron now spoke forcefully. 'I stick by them – always have, always will.'

The gentleman doth protest too much, Kendrick thought. 'That's it, then, and I don't need to bother you any longer.'

'Are you telling what all this is about?'

'Routine enquiries.'

'You come here to make routine enquiries on a Sunday morning?'

'There's no peace for the wicked.'

'And there ain't any for the honest, when the likes of you comes around.'

Kendrick walked into the CID general room. Myers, seated at his desk, the only other person present, looked up. 'Finally honouring us with your presence?'

'Things took time.'

'Always do when you're as sharp as a Swiss admiral.'

'The chap on duty at Hallam House put me on to Cameron, who was the bank guard Friday night. He was asleep, so I had to wait.'

'So there was two of you having trouble waking up. What did he have to say?'

Kendrick sat on the desk. 'Came on duty at six, made a round at ten past that was completed by about half past, sat at the control desk from which he had a clear view of the main entrance until nine. He didn't see Penfold leave soon after seven.'

'Surprise, surprise! So him leaving the office at seven was all balls, like I've always said it was. He left much earlier, tanked up in a pub and then, still feeling thirsty, emptied the bottle of whisky and after that didn't know which of him was driving.'

'Where did he drink the whisky?'

'You need a prompt screen? Didn't he tell he was in the lay-by? Isn't that where you found the bottle cap?'

'I don't see it.'

'Like most times, you can't see beyond the end of your nose.'

'He's just not the kind of man to stop in a lay-by and booze.'

'You want to know what his kind is? Hypocrites, telling everyone what honest, decent people they are when most of the time they're crawling around in the gutters.'

'And not looking up at the stars?'

'How's that?'

'Nothing . . . Dave, I just don't think it fits.'

'You just don't think . . . Why d'you keep trying to fly his flag? Because you haven't learned yet that being rich doesn't mean you're worth anything?'

'There has to be an explanation for his not having been seen leaving at seven – which means there wasn't reasonable time for him to get drunk.'

'If the guard didn't see him, then he didn't leave when he said he did. Unless he can make himself invisible.'

'I reckon it's likely that's what Cameron did.'

'He went for a quick fly to Mars?'

'He became uneasy when I started questioning him about whether he could have slipped away from the control desk and not made an entry in the log. He's not supposed to leave it between the first round and the next one at nine. But if he thought there was no one left in the building, he maybe made himself a cup of tea at around seven. If I'm right . . .'

'If elephants started flying, we'd all need bloody large umbrellas.'

'Dave, no one has yet been able to suggest why Penfold offers evidence he must recognize sounds utterly absurd – unless it's because that's the truth.'

'I told you why.'

'But that . . . Sometimes, you kind of slam down the shutters because of the chip on your shoulder.'

'Which is a sight better than having blinkers over the eyes.'

Kendrick shrugged his shoulders. He looked up at the clock on the wall. 'Is the canteen still serving lunch?'

'On a Sunday?'

'Then I'm off to a pub for some grub.'

'And if I say you aren't because there's paperwork to finish?'

'I'll suggest a use for it. If you haven't eaten yet, how about joining me?'

'Being Sunday, I brought something from home.'

Vinegar sandwiches, Kendrick decided, as he turned and left.

Nine

'I hate leaving Charles behind,' Lucy said.

Penfold slowed for an oncoming car and then turned left. 'You're afraid he pines for home?'

'He looked so downcast when we left.'

'Most likely, the after-effects of two chocolate mousses.'

She was silent for a while, then said, 'Do you think he blames us for sending him to boarding school – thinks we've abandoned him?'

He took his left hand off the wheel and momentarily touched her arm in a quick gesture of comforting affection. 'I had a word with Potts – or Botts; I'm never quite certain which – and he said that when there was good-natured devilment going on, he was never surprised to find Charles in the thick of it.'

'You're trying to say that shows he's happy? It could be because he's so unhappy.'

'No kid who was unhappy could be so buoyant as he was today right up until we were about to leave. If he were really unhappy, he'd be a loner.'

'I do hope you're right . . . I sometimes wonder why we send our children away to school.'

'To maintain tradition, of course.'

'That's not funny.'

'Sorry. Only I'm certain you're worrying unnecessarily.'

They came up to a small car trailing a caravan and he drew out to overtake before remembering Lucy's Astra lacked the Jaguar's acceleration; an oncoming car forced him to draw back into the nearside. 'I wonder how much longer the police are going to keep the Jag?'

They rounded a corner to enter a mile-long straight stretch of road and he was finally able to overtake. On either side, the land was flat, virtually treeless, and the fields large because one of the many mistaken governmental agricultural policies of the past had been to rip out hedges. With a heavily overcast sky and the light beginning to fade, it was a melancholy landscape.

'I think we should have mentioned something,' he said. 'Dropped a hint that there could be trouble.'

'A hint could have left his believing things were much worse than they are; he'd have had to hear the full story.'

'Could things be much worse?'

'Why do you say that?'

'If the police were satisfied I was telling the truth, by now they'd surely have returned the car? We haven't heard a word from them.'

'Which must be a good omen.'

A short while before, he'd been trying to ease her fears; now she was trying to ease his. He hoped he'd been the more successful. 'I'd have expected them to get back on to me to find out if I could give them any more information about the men who grabbed me.'

'They know you've told them all you can.'

'I've always understood that it's part of their technique to go on and on asking questions in the hopes of making one recall memories one didn't know one had. With the poor woman in hospital, I'd have expected them to—'

'Why are you talking like this?'

'If things start becoming really nasty, there'll be publicity and the school will learn about it. Kids can be cruel tormentors.'

'Stop it, Gavin.'

'We have to face the facts.'

'The fact is, you've told the police the truth, so they'll

never be able to prove you were driving the car when the woman was hit.'

The truth can be a poor shield, he thought.

He crossed to the Regency inlaid commode that had been converted – not at his instigation – into a cocktail cabinet, opened the right-hand door, brought out a bottle of gin and one of tonic, poured himself another drink. As he returned to his chair, he said, 'Don't worry, it's my last this evening.'

'I wasn't worrying.'

Was that the truth? He couldn't judge, even after many years of marriage. He sat. His was always a stressful job, but in the past there had been a breach of security which had proved very difficult to identify; senior management had become unable to understand the magnitude of the task even when this had been explained to them in detail. Professional pride, as much as their impatient ignorance, had caused him more and more frequently to seek the false optimism and temporary release from pressure that alcohol offered. He'd ignored her hints that he was drinking ever more heavily and had only recognized the dangers when, after a very difficult time at the office, they'd had a meal at her parents' home and he had become argumentatively obnoxious and finally plain drunk. Remorse had provided the will to regain self-control . . . Small wonder that when she had come out of the house to find him drunk in the car, she had initially believed he had broken his promise, made the day following that disastrous visit; small wonder that now she was dreading stress would once more . . .

'Don't you believe me?' she suddenly asked.

'Of course I do.'

Clemens stood in front of the desk and resentfully wondered why the DI seldom suggested he sat when making his morning report; it seemed so petty a way of underlining rank.

'No word from the lab regarding the whisky bottle and cap?' Ingham asked.

'Not yet, sir.'

'Or from the supermarkets?'

'They said they were doing all they could, but it would take time to separate out the information we've asked for.'

'A hallowed British excuse for immobility. I gather the security guard at Hallam House says Penfold did not leave the building soon after seven that evening?'

'He's quite definite. The only thing is . . .'

'Well?'

'Kendrick believes Cameron was lying when claiming he wasn't away from the control desk at the relevant times.'

'His reason for that belief?'

'Hasn't any. Describes it as an impression.'

'So how much weight do we put on his impression?'

'Difficult to say.'

'I'm asking you to say.'

Clemens spoke resentfully. 'As I've mentioned before, sir, Myers says he's inclined to be very imaginative.'

'Imagination isn't always erroneous. However, detail someone else to question Cameron again. On second thoughts, you can do that . . . Could Penfold have left the building by another exit?'

'All emergency exits are one-way, covered by CCTVs and alarms. Had he tried to leave by one, control would have been alerted; and in any case, that's against company rules.'

How typical, Ingham thought, that Clemens should imagine company rules alone would prove a deterrent to a quick route home. 'Have the video tapes been checked to find out if Penfold managed to leave without triggering the alarm?'

'I don't think so.'

'You should know so. See it's done as soon as possible. What about a camera covering the main entrance?'

'There is one, but it's switched off at night as an economy measure, except when the guard's making his rounds.'

'The bank's motto must be, Penny wise, pound foolish. And we put our money in their hands for safety! . . . How's Mrs Lynch today?'

'I spoke to the hospital earlier and they say she's making a good recovery, but as yet there's no date for her discharge.'

'Is she fit enough to be questioned?'

'I gather so.'

'Get that done. And someone must have another word with the eyewitness – What's her name?'

'Mrs Fenella Gill.'

'Right. One last thing: have you detailed someone to question the staff at the pubs Penfold would be likely to visit near Hallam House or on his drive home?'

'Yes, sir.'

'We need results quickly. I've heard the local rag is about to run a campaign against bad driving, so the last thing we want is to give them the ammunition for blaming us for failing to identify a drunken driver guilty of injuring an elderly woman.'

DC Ernest Young was well named, being of an earnest nature. He spoke to a nurse who directed him to the end bed, by the window. He introduced himself, handed Muriel Lynch the small bunch of red roses he had bought from the barrow set up near the main entrance to the hospital.

She smiled with pleasure, told him roses were her favourite flower and explained at length why this was. He feigned interest as he listened, seated on the chair between the beds. Eventually he managed to say he would like to ask her some questions. 'Mrs Lynch, will you—'

'Be a dear boy and find something to put these lovely roses in.'

He spoke to a nurse, who went into an office and brought out a plastic vase into which she'd put some water. He returned to the bed and set the vase on the locker.

'I'm so glad you're here, because I'm terribly worried,' she said.

'Why's that?'

'You see, we've never before been separated, even for one night, and Elvira will be very upset.'

He suggested asking a woman police constable to call at the house to see what help she could offer before being told that Elvira was a nine-year-old cat. It was true a neighbour had promised to feed her every day, and tell her Mother would soon be back, but . . .

'I'm sure your neighbour is looking after her perfectly. Now if . . .'

'I got her soon after my dear husband died. He was always upset by cats – they made him sneeze and sneeze – so I couldn't have one when he was alive . . . Do you like cats?'

'Yes. What I need to know—'

'I always say that people who like cats must be nice people and it's true. Have you noticed that? Of course, it's not the same with dogs. Quite nasty people have dogs.'

Eventually he was able to ask her what she remembered about the accident. She had stepped off the pavement, a car had come round the corner very, very quickly and knocked her flying. She'd suffered a lot of pain, but the ambulance men had been wonderful and the nurses couldn't be kinder, except for the one who didn't like cats and called them smelly, spiteful animals . . .

Young braked the CID Rover to a halt in front of number 16, a semi-detached in a road of semi-detacheds, all built between the wars. He opened the metal gate and walked up the short brick path, past a handkerchief-size lawn and a rose bed in which each plant had been carefully pruned and not a weed grew. The porch had little depth; the front door was wooden except that in the upper quarter there was a crudely designed marine scene in stained glass.

The door was opened by an elderly man whose girth

evidenced an overfed, immobile life and which, Young judged, disqualified him as the keen gardener. 'Mr Gill?'

'That's me?' His answer was also a question.

'Detective Constable Young, county CID.' He showed his warrant card.

'Come about the accident, I suppose. When she came home and told me what had happened . . . Here, don't stand there; come on inside.'

Young stepped into a short, narrow hall, made smaller by an elaborate hallstand.

'Mind you, I had something to say about her being out at that time of night on her own! When she said she'd be taking some things to Dora, who was ill, I said, You wait until I get back so as I can drive you there. Isn't safe to be out on the streets these days.'

Gill called out to his wife, then opened the first door on his right, led the way into an immaculately tidy sitting room and, once they were seated, recounted the story of his friend who had gone up to London and been mugged in the morning, had returned to Folkestone in the afternoon and been knocked over by a couple of young hooligans on skateboards. Small wonder people were saying there was no longer any law and order . . .

Fenella Gill entered, and as Young stood, he thought that their marriage was one of opposites. She was thin and full of nervous energy; as she said hullo, she quickly plumped a cushion on the nearest chair.

'I'm sorry to bother you, Mrs Gill . . .' Young began.

'That's all right. I've prepared lunch and I'm not going out until this afternoon.'

'Going out where?' Gill asked.

'The crochet class. I told you they've been changed to Mondays.'

'I can't think why you bother.'

'Because I want to learn to crochet well.'

'Why, when you do so much knitting?'

She didn't bother to answer – spoke to Young. 'You want to know about the dreadful accident on Friday, I suppose? First you can tell me how Muriel is today. I haven't had the chance to visit the hospital this morning and when one phones, one never seems to get through.'

'She's continuing to make a satisfactory recovery.'

'When I saw her lying in the road, I feared she was far more seriously injured than, thankfully, she was. The poor woman was born under an unlucky star. It's hardly a year since she slipped and broke her wrist. As my mother used to say: some people are born accident-prone. I know someone who was in hospital four times in six months because of accidents.' She moved the small lamp on the table by her side one inch to the right.

A sparrow, Young thought: restless, chirpy, occasionally aggressive. 'Perhaps you'll tell me what you remember about the accident?'

She interleaved her fingers, rested her hands on her lap; almost immediately, she unlocked them to smooth down an already smooth arm of the loose cover. 'I'd taken some food to Dora . . .'

'I told you to wait,' Gill said, 'so as I could drive you.'

'And spend an hour or more doing nothing because you were still at the Lord Nelson with all your drinking friends? . . . I gave Dora the stew, had a chat, because she gets so lonely, and was returning, when I saw someone on the other side step on to the road as a car, travelling very fast, came round that dreadful corner where there have been two other accidents I can remember.'

'Can you judge what speed it was doing?'

'All I can say is that the tyres were squealing.'

'You definitely heard that?'

'I'd hardly say I did if I didn't.'

'Of course not, but I do have to make absolutely certain, because it could well be an important piece of evidence . . . Did you actually see the car hit Mrs Lynch?'

'I did and it was truly shocking.'

'I'm sure it was. Yet you bravely managed to overcome the shock and record the car's registration number . . .'

'Bravery had nothing to do with it,' she said sharply. 'It was my duty. Unfortunately, I couldn't read the last letter because I wasn't wearing my distance glasses.'

'What you were able to tell us was of very great value.'

'Then you've been able to identify the car?'

'We think so . . . I believe you said it was a Jaguar?'

'You must know it is if you've found it.'

'You are interested in cars?'

'No. I dislike them because of all the harm they cause. But an acquaintance of ours owns a Jaguar and he can never stop telling everyone how wonderful it is. Of course, he does that to try to make us appreciate he can afford an expensive car.'

'I don't think that's really fair,' Gill said.

'Neither he nor Mary can ever stop showing off. Naturally, they're far less keen to say where the money comes from.'

'Do you think you should say things like that in front of a policeman?'

'Why not?'

'I can be very deaf,' Young said hastily. 'So your acquaintance owns a Jaguar, which means you know what one looks like and that's why you were able to identify the make of car that knocked down Mrs Lynch?'

'Yes.'

'Do you know what model Jaguar your acquaintance owns?'

'No.'

'It's an XK-8,' Gill said.

'Are you certain?' she asked aggressively.

'He's told me often enough.'

Once more, Young redirected the conversation. 'After it had knocked Mrs Lynch down, you say it drove off in an easterly direction?'

'I've no idea whether it was easterly or westerly. All I can say is, it continued just as quickly, as if absolutely nothing had happened.'

Young closed his notebook. 'Thank you. You've been very helpful.'

'I'm so very annoyed I wasn't wearing my distance glasses, because then I'd have been able to read the last letter and make certain whether it really *was* someone.'

'I don't quite understand.'

'What don't you understand?'

'What you meant when you said you would have been able to see if it *was* someone.'

'After I couldn't read the last letter, I looked up and thought a person was peering through the back window of the car as it raced away.'

'But you can't be certain of that?'

'All I could make out was a shape which did seem to be a face, but the car was just too far away for me to be sure.'

How big a cat was that going to put amongst the pigeons? Young wondered.

Ten

'Was it or was it not a face?' Ingham said.
Young remained silent.

'She says she looked up and saw this shape – so the car was further away than when she'd been unable to read the whole of the registration number.'

'But if it was a face . . .'

'I don't need to be told what that would mean.' He picked up a pencil and momentarily seemed about to snap it in two.

'She said it was so much like a face, it's difficult to think what else it could have been.'

'When motorists are daft enough to have fluffy animals dancing up and down on strings over their rear windows? Was anything of that nature in the back of the Jaguar?'

'Can't say, sir.'

Ingham searched amongst the papers on his desk, picked up one to read. 'Then you'll be pleased to know that the answer is: not.'

'Since he must have been too far gone to realize there might be a point in removing something . . .'

'His wife has the necessary character and intelligence to work out that a face would offer advantages a bouncy dog would not, and may have removed the dog.'

'When she almost certainly had no reason to know her husband was in serious trouble until we called and told her?'

'Do you have any more penetrating observations you'd like to make?'

80

'Only trying to think things through, sir.'

'That's my job.'

And is it one you're cursing? Young thought.

Bonner entered the Four Feathers – the fifth public house he'd visited – and noting it served real ale, ordered a half of bitter. It would have been poor PR to ask for information and not buy a drink. When the glass was empty, he signalled to the barman, who nodded as he served two men who stood at the end of the bar.

Two blondes – one just possibly genuine – came through the doorway and sat at the table nearest the window. The older had the type of looks that had always attracted him in a hurry, and he was about to cross and speak to them when two bikers entered and strutted with youthful cockiness to their table; one sat, the other went to the bar. Bonner sighed.

The barman came up to where he stood. 'How are things with you?' he asked.

'Could be worse, I suppose.'

'If you was in my job, they sure as hell would be . . . Does the name Gavin Penfold talk to you?'

'Don't think so.'

'Six foot or maybe a sliver over, well built, light-brown hair with a bit of a wave, blue eyes, a solid nose, well spoken, and the look of someone who'll tell you just what to do if you get in his way. A little old for steaming up a car in a country lane, but still interested. Drives a silver Jaguar and is with the Counties Bank.'

'We've one or two come in who work for that outfit, but your description doesn't ring any bells.'

'Might have been here Friday night – say between six and seven – emptying his glass as fast as he could swallow.'

'Sorry.'

'No cause for sackcloth and ashes. Beer's as good as ever.'

'You asking for a refill on the house?'
'Now there's a generous idea!'

Penfold replaced the receiver, leaned back in the chair and stared unseeingly across the room in which six of the other work stations were manned. Bampton, one of his agents, said an international banking company wanted a security network architect with the qualifications he possessed and were offering a salary just short of twice what he was presently receiving. According to Bampton, if his name was put forward, the job was his. He'd said to go ahead. He enjoyed his present work, but not only would there be the greatly increased salary; the position would enhance his standing in the computer world . . . Last Christmas he had pulled a cracker with Charles and the major portion had been his; out of it had come a paper hat and, on a slip of paper with crudely printed holly and bells, the aphorism, 'The blacker life appears to be, the lighter it can become' – at the time dismissed as pretentious nonsense; now, words remembered because they might hold the hope that soon he would be believed . . .

Since he had put in so much overtime recently, identifying and erasing a fault due to human error, there was little reason why he should not return home earlier than usual, tell Lucy about the probability of the new job and take her out to dinner at her favourite restaurant, where the food and service had not yet deteriorated following favourable publicity. For the first time for a long while, he enjoyed the warmth of optimism. Soon the police would finally admit he had been telling the truth and that they had been too hidebound to understand the difference between unlikely and impossible.

As Clemens climbed the stairs in Seacrest House, each flight taken at a slower pace, he uneasily wondered if breathlessness was just the unavoidable consequence of age or also the herald of something serious. Only that morning there had been an article in the paper about the prevalence of heart disease in the country.

He rang the bell of flat 11c. The door was opened by Cameron, who stared at him with a not-buying-anything expression. 'Detective Sergeant Clemens, county CID. I'd like a word, if that's OK?'

'And if it ain't?'

'I won't keep you long.'

'That's right, you won't.'

Surly bastard, he thought, unaware that there were those in CID who would have described him in similar terms.

Cameron led the way into the sitting room, where he slumped down on the settee. Clemens sat on an armchair and stared at the opened magazine, face downwards on the floor. Molly would never have allowed such untidiness . . .

'Are you spending the rest of the afternoon saying nowt?' Cameron asked.

'You spoke to a colleague yesterday . . .'

'Work all night, home for a real good kip and what happens? Get woken up and asked a lot of daft questions.'

'Necessary questions, because we're investigating a serious incident . . . You told PC Kendrick you go on duty at six, make your first round almost immediately, the next at nine, and between those times you're not to take a tea break. Is that right?'

'Yeah.'

'And if you have to leave the control desk for whatever reason and for however short a time, you have to note the fact down in the log?'

'So?'

'On Friday evening, you didn't make tea or take a toilet break after the end of your six o'clock round and before your nine o'clock one?'

'There'd have been a log entry, wouldn't there, if I had of done.'

'Would there?'

'Trying to call me a liar?'

It would have been a pleasure, but hardly the way to gain co-operation. 'Look, mate, let's forget the rules and regulations, which are a load of balls at the best of times. We both know how things work in the real world. You need a Jimmy, you take one, because a man has to do what he has to do; you want a cup of tea to put some life into you, you make one, and since there've been no alarms, where's the harm if the log remains blank?'

'I don't work like that.'

'What you tell me now doesn't even get whispered anywhere else.'

'Why are you asking?'

'If you did leave the control desk, just for a minute, someone could have left the building without you seeing him.'

'Who's the someone? Mr Penfold?'

'Why suggest him?'

'That's who the other detective was talking about. . . So why bother if I did or didn't see him?'

'We'll need to ask you a few questions.'

'Ain't that what you're doing now?'

'Different questions.'

'And there'll be trouble?'

'There's no saying that.'

'And you're not saying there won't. So if you thinks I'd tell something what could cost me my job, you're off your trolley.'

'It could mean a great deal to someone.'

'That's his problem.'

'It wouldn't worry you, knowing that what you said might help him, but if you keep silent, he could be in the shit?'

'I was at the control desk from after the first round until the nine o'clock one and there's the log to say that's fact.'

As Clemens went down the stairs, he decided Kendrick was right and Cameron was a liar – but it was going to be very difficult to prove this.

*   *   *

The forensic laboratory made a preliminary report by phone.

'The nine-centimetre length of woollen thread is similar in all respects to the material of which the dress is made.'

'So it definitely came from Mrs Lynch's dress?' Myers asked.

'We're saying,' the speaker repeated in weary tones, 'that it is similar in all respects. It is very probable it did come from that dress, but we are unable to say beyond any doubt that it did.'

'What are the odds against it coming from another dress?'

'One needs to know how many dresses were made from the same batch of material before one can give an accurate opinion.'

'Can't you find wherever the thread was torn from?'

'We can identify where the dress has been jagged and material is missing. We cannot say for certain that the missing thread is the exhibit thread.'

'If you meet a man wearing a halo and walking on water, do you have to examine the halo before you acknowledge he's a saint.'

'Should such circumstances arise, ask me again.'

'What about the pattern on the car's paintwork?'

'Very difficult to determine with sufficient accuracy, but we can go so far as to say it is consistent with the pattern that would be made by the frock if it were worn by someone who was thrown up on to the bonnet of the car.'

'But not if someone else was wearing it?'

'What's that supposed to mean?'

Myers did not explain. His little jokes were seldom appreciated because, he was convinced, so few people had a sense of humour. 'What about the bottle?'

'We received it from Dabs. As you'll know, the cap on this type of bottle is so secured that it fractures when it's twisted. The fracturing causes patterns of stress and usually these can be identified for comparison under magnification. We can say that the cap came from the bottle.'

'No maybes or perhapses?'

'No comment.'

'Can you tell us anything more?

'No.'

'You'll forward a written report as soon as possible?'

The line was cut. Myers studied what he'd written. He dialled the Finger-print Section, spoke to a woman who said she'd check the notes of the case. Phone to ear, he stared across at the group photograph of CID, C division, taken many years before and left hanging on the wall in spite of the fact that none of those pictured were still working locally. He wondered what had happened to them? Retired? They were to be envied. Dead? Perhaps they also should be envied . . .

'Sorry to keep you waiting, but the notes had gone for a walk.'

'Don't they always when you most want them!' He tried to be amusingly friendly with the ladies, in spite of his wife's judgement that when he did so, he tended to sound old-man lecherous.

'There is only the one set of prints. We think it likely the bottle was wiped clean before the prints became impressed.'

'You can't be more definite?'

'I'm afraid not.'

If one had an overactive imagination, one could recognize the possibility that here was further weak corroborative evidence of Penfold's story. A bottle bought in a supermarket must have other prints on it because it had been stacked on a shelf; a villain, unless greener than April grass, would have wiped the bottle down, for fear of leaving any of his own traces, before imposing Penfold's prints. On the other hand, if one favoured common sense over imagination, the bottle had been wiped down because it had been dirty when Penfold bought it and he had cleaned it before storing it in his car for future, furtive use . . .

'Are you still there?'

'Sorry. I was thinking.'

'One more thing: the prints are from the left hand.'

Was Penfold left-handed? Did that matter? A man desperate for a drink wasn't going to give a damn with which hand he rushed a bottle to his mouth.

The call finished, he went through to the DI's room, but Ingham was still not there. He wrote another report and put it with the first one on the middle of the large, elaborately tooled leather blotter on the desk. An image-promoter, Myers sourly judged that to be.

Eleven

They left the restaurant and crossed the car park to the Astra. After opening the front passenger door for Lucy, Penfold went round the bonnet, settled behind the wheel. 'I take it we head for home?'

'Not yet. I don't want the evening to end; it's so wonderful seeing you happy once more and knowing I'm going to be able to boast about the wonderful new job my husband has.'

'You've always said how much you dislike boasting.'

'So I do, when it's other women boasting about their husbands.'

He laughed.

'Are you in a forgiving mood?'

'Being a cautious man, I'm not sure.'

'Not even on a special night?'

'It's so unusual for you to need to be forgiven for anything, I have the feeling you've committed something heinous.'

'And there'll be no forgiveness?'

'Now I'm very nervous indeed. Just what have you been up to?'

'I rang Charles at school because I was so worried . . . I know you've often said we shouldn't keep getting in touch with him as some mother-hens do, but I just had to know how he was.'

'And he told you he was fine, and when you said he looked so downhearted when we left, he explained he'd been remembering that the next full-day exeat was a month away, so he'd have to be on starvation diet until then.'

'Are you psychic?'

'Possibly.'

'But unlikely, because you're the wrong kind of character. I believe you knew damn well what he might have said to me because you rang him from work and he said the same thing to you.'

'As always, too acute for a simpleton like myself. I confess. *Mea culpa.*'

'And you weren't going to tell me?'

'There was no need.'

'Not knowing I was so worried . . .'

'No need when I knew that you knew he was all right.'

'How could you?'

'When I spoke to the dragon at the school and said I wanted a word with Charles, she lectured me on the problems caused by parents who continually phoned and interrupted the routine and this was the second time today she'd had to find him . . . If I were not so frightened of female dragons, I'd have pointed out that if the school did not have a ban on mobiles, there would be no upset routines.'

'I'll try and forgive you your deception.'

'On the principle that the best form of defence is attack?'

'Anyway, I'm very relieved Charles says he's in good spirits.'

'As I suggested yesterday that he was.'

'If you were so certain, why did you bother to phone today?'

'I decided that the only way in which to convince you was to be able to tell you I'd spoken to him.'

'You're a liar, aren't you?'

'How can a man have a happy marriage if he isn't?'

'You're insufferable this evening!'

'Blame the bottle of Margaux.' He started the engine. 'If we're not heading home, where are we going?'

'Down to the sea wall at Barkstone.'

'For any particular reason?'

'You have to ask?' she said incredulously. Then, thanks to the outside lights, she saw he was smiling. 'You're being a real bastard! I can't think why I love you so.' She kissed him, settled back, fixed the seat belt.

'This is a nostalgic return to the past?' he said, as he drove out on to the road.

'No objections, I hope?'

'One.'

'Now what are you going to say in the mistaken belief it's humorous?'

'That I hope the nostalgic past is not to be exactly repeated.'

'Why not?'

'After I'd proposed and you'd accepted, we returned – since this was back in the Dark Ages – to our respective, chaste, single beds.'

'One of the things that so attracted me was, you didn't seem to realize that for most people, the permissive age had arrived.' She put her arm across the back of his seat, rested her fingertips against his neck. 'Of course, one can be chaste in a double bed. If one wants to be.'

On Tuesday morning Clemens entered the DI's room exactly on nine o'clock. 'Morning, sir.'

'What's the night report?' Ingham asked briskly, not bothering to return the greeting.

'One break-in and one mugging in town, a serious three-vehicle accident on the motorway just inside the division, a couple of domestics, a farm fire that might be arson, a pub brawl in Westry, and a missing person report from Richmouth. All in hand, either with uniform or us. There's some doubt whether the fourteen-year-old daughter really is missing or has taken herself off to friends and not let her family know. Soper is checking on that.'

'I want to hear as soon as we have any news.'

'Sir.'

'Have you questioned Cameron?'

'Yesterday afternoon.'

'Draw up a chair and tell me about it.'

Clemens, concealing his surprise at this relaxation of formal procedure, picked up one of the wooden chairs by the wall, set it in front of the desk and sat. 'I went to his place and explained we were checking certain facts, and asked him if there was any chance he might have left the control desk on Friday night and was away for so short a time he didn't bother to make an entry in the log. He was adamant: no way.'

'Did you believe him?'

'He's a difficult character to read, but I'd say he's lying because if he did leave the desk and not log the fact, he'd be in right royal trouble.'

'Surely you told him that anything he said would go no further?'

'He wasn't buying that. He'd guessed from Kendrick there was serious trouble brewing and so knew that whatever promises he was given, there had to be the chance of what he said coming out in the open.'

'In other words, you failed to gain his confidence.'

Thanks very much, Clemens silently said.

'Why didn't you believe him?'

'There was nothing concrete to go on, but like Kendrick, I just felt he was lying. At a guess, he wanted a cup of tea or coffee and "forgot" to log his absence from the desk. But he's not going to admit that now for fear of the consequences.'

'Suppose he's leaned on?'

'I'd say he's someone who'll react to pressure by becoming ever more stubbornly unco-operative.'

Ingham was silent for a moment, then said, 'Has someone spoken to the staff at the pubs?'

'Bonner's covered them. No one remembers Penfold drinking on Friday evening.'

'Which doesn't mean he wasn't in one of 'em.' Ingham picked up a pencil, fiddled with it, inadvertently broke the lead, swore and dropped it. 'There's a lot riding on Cameron.

If Penfold was at Hallam House until seven and left unob-
served because Cameron was making tea, then realistically
there just wasn't time for him to get blind drunk even if he
had a bottle of whisky in the car. If he left considerably earlier
– say, when the majority of employees packed up – then he
had the time to down a lot of alcohol . . . I want the staff
at the bank to be questioned to find out if any of them saw
Penfold leave work on Friday.'

'That'll take a lot of manpower . . .'

'There's no need to point out the obvious.' He picked up
the pencil once more. 'Why would a man in his position drive
into a lay-by and booze there rather than returning home and
drinking in comfort?'

'If he's an alcoholic, his wife could be at him so much he
does most of his drinking out of sight.'

'Which would probably only conceal it until he reached
home. Or is that to grant an alcoholic a sense of logic he
probably doesn't have? Hunt around for any evidence of
heavy drinking.'

'Until he's charged, that could be dicey and, given half
a chance, I'll bet he'd complain hard and long about an
intrusion into his private life.'

'Make certain he's not given the chance.' There was a silence,
which Ingham finally broke. 'This case is giving me a lot of
grief. Before I send papers through to the CPS in a serious
case, I always like to try to see the facts as the defence will
present them, because that can reveal loopholes which need
plugging. They'll be unable to deny it was Penfold's car that
bowled the woman over in Oak Cross; that when we arrived at
Alten Cobb, he was paralytic; that his wife admits she saw no
one else, heard no car drive off. So they'll counter the obvious
assumption that he was driving the Jaguar when Mrs Lynch was
hit by presenting his version of events. On the face of things,
not even a half-witted jury is going to believe such nonsense,
but they will claim that its very absurdity proves its veracity.
Which raises the question: what was the motive for snatching

him and making him drunk? He'll have to expand his theory that it is in some way connected with his job at the bank. Could that be possible? I think we should admit that where money's concerned, anything's possible. Accept that the men who grabbed him intended to use him in some scam, why did they make him tight and drop him at his home? Because the woman had been hit and injured, and they realized that if the car's identity had been noted, we'd be crowding Penfold so quickly they wouldn't have the time to make use of him . . . How do we counter that possibility?'

'Do we have to? Like you said: no jury's going to think his story worth believing.'

'He has the money to brief a top silk. A clever barrister can even bamboozle a jury into imagining they understand what's going on . . . Has there been anything yet from the supermarkets?'

'Not a word. They did say it would probably prove impossible to trace the sale of a single bottle.'

'Not impossible, but it would take time and effort that offered no profit – only our thanks . . . I want evidence, positive or negative, of Penfold's drinking habits. And let's pray that Soper finds the girl is with friends and not lying in a ditch, having been raped and strangled.'

Clemens knocked and entered the DI's office in the late afternoon on Thursday.

'They need an accountant for my job,' Ingham said, as he looked up.

'Trouble with the budget, sir?'

'How do you make five quid do the work of twenty; cut overtime when we need more working hours; provide better clear-up rates when that takes time and time is money? . . . So what's your problem?'

'I put Bonner on to finding out about Penfold's drink-ing habits.'

'Set a thief to catch a thief?'

'He's good at getting people to talk.'

'So how talkative have they been?'

'No joy with Penfold's gardener and daily – both very tight-lipped – but he learned Mrs Penfold's parents live not far away and decided to try there. The Groves employ a part-time gardener, Menzies, so Bonner made contact at a pub. After a pint or two, and some subtle prompting, Menzies let on that Penfold had a problem with drink. One time, Menzies was doing some weeding by an open window and heard Mrs Groves telling Mrs Penfold that if her husband didn't ease up on drinking, he could be in trouble. Not long afterwards, Penfold got so tight during a meal that there was a scene and when he left, his wife was driving and he didn't know whether it was day or night.'

'That could just be the weight to tilt the scales, if prosecuting counsel has the wit to know how to slide the evidence into court.'

'Do we arrest Penfold?'

'We'll have him in for one more interview and see how things run. Send someone along to Hallam House to ask him to come here.'

'We don't wait to speak to him at his home?'

'And miss the opportunity of unsettling him because he'll know that he'll have become a marked man at work?'

Penfold was reading a report when Mercer threaded his way between the work tables and came to a halt by his side. 'There's someone wants a word with you, Gavin.'

'Who?'

'Detective Constable Young.'

Tension seemed to tighten his chest.

'Very politely professional; showed me his warrant card. So what have you been up to?'

'I must have parked on a solid line.'

Mercer was, as ever, pedantically precise. 'I'm fairly certain detectives aren't concerned with traffic matters.'

But they were when a woman was badly injured by a car that was being driven recklessly.

Penfold left the high-security area, went up the short flight of stairs and through to the atrium, crossing to where a man whose face reminded him of a disliked uncle stood by the side of a potted aspidistra.

'Mr Penfold?' Young said.

'Yes.'

'DC Young . . . I'd like to ask you to come to divisional HQ as soon as possible.'

'Why?'

'To help in our enquiries into an incident last Friday in which an elderly woman was knocked down by a car that didn't stop.'

'I've given all the information I can.' He glanced at the young woman behind the reception desk and she, less attractive than she believed, hurriedly looked away. She was within earshot and must have heard every word. The rumours would spring into life like dragon's teeth.

'Nevertheless, the detective inspector would be grateful if you would come along.'

'When?'

'As soon as possible,' Young patiently repeated.

'I need to consult my solicitor.'

'Perhaps when you've done so, you'll phone to say when you expect to arrive?'

'If he advises me to do so.'

'Then I will report back to the detective inspector that you've kindly said you'll come to the station very soon.'

Mercer should have added, Penfold thought, that Young's politeness was of a professionally hypocritical nature.

Twelve

Waite possessed the talents that a good country solicitor should: he was friendly, discreet, preferred compromise to confrontation, possessed a reasonable knowledge of the law and sound common sense rather than brilliant intellect. In his middle forties, he retained the handsome features which, when unmarried, had made him a popular escort at hunt balls.

He tapped his artistically long fingers on the eighteenth-century pedestal desk – inherited from the previous senior partner. 'It is a somewhat unusual set of circumstances . . .'

'Which happen to be true,' Penfold said sharply.

'Of course.' He stopped tapping. 'The problem is, people find it difficult to accept that truth really can be stranger than fiction and policemen are not noted for broad and receptive minds.'

'You're saying they'll continue to find it difficult to believe I'm not lying?'

'They may well take some convincing. Unfortunately, from what you've told me, you are not in a position to offer solid proof of the truth.'

'It's difficult to offer anything when you're blindfolded, gagged, bound, shoved between the seats of a car and finally made to drink yourself stupid.'

'Indeed . . . You cannot suggest a more precise motive for their actions?'

'Only what I've said.'

'You've no idea what form of fraud or theft they had been hoping to perpetrate with your enforced help?'

'All I know is, it must have involved a breach of security.'

'Have you recently been approached by anyone who, in the light of hindsight, acted suspiciously or out of character?'

'No.'

'As network architect, I presume you are in possession of considerable sensitive information?'

'I could foul up the whole of the bank's operations.'

'Or benefit someone financially?'

'In double spades. But apart from the fact that I wouldn't do something illegal, I'd know that it must eventually become obvious what I'd done.'

'Which wouldn't, of course, be of any concern to those who forced you to act . . . It could be a difficult course to take, to press that point home, but I imagine it is quite possible it is one which counsel will decide on.'

'Are you saying I'm likely to be arrested?'

'Quite clearly, the police believe you were drunk and driving the car that hit Mrs Lynch in Oak Cross. If they can assemble sufficient evidence to support that belief and the CPS considers this strong enough, yes, I'm afraid I think it very likely you will be arrested and put on trial.'

'When I wasn't capable of driving a pedal car?' Penfold said wildly.

'One has to accept that humans do not have a divine omniscience, so circumstances can determine that an innocent man is tried for a crime he did not commit. Thankfully, our system of independent justice ensures that few – very few indeed – who are innocent are wrongly found guilty.'

'Not much consolation for the few.'

'Of course not. And I'm not suggesting that you are likely to suffer so unjustly . . . I think it would be a good idea if I phone now and say we're on our way. That will make it clear we are offering the fullest co-operation; of course, were we on the Continent, I would proffer different advice because there, co-operation is taken as a sign of guilt.' He smiled.

'But do you think . . .' Penfold stopped, accepting Waite

97

was too much of a diplomat to give an honest opinion. 'I'd like to phone Lucy.'

'Of course. You can do so in here; the phone nearer the window is the outside line. I'll go downstairs and get in touch with the police, then wait by reception. Just one more thing: I imagine Detective Inspector Ingham will conduct the interview. Basically, he is straightforward, but he's also ambitious, sharp, and looking for a good internal CV to help promotion, and that requires as many cases solved as possible. So you need to keep any chance of a solid case well out of his reach. Restrict yourself to facts; if he insinuates, don't become riled; use humour to disarm.' Waite stood, left the room, his brisk strides those of a man who was physically fit.

Penfold dialled home. Agnes, the daily, answered and said she'd fetch Mrs Penfold. Agnes had borne two children, fathered by different men, both of whom had deserted her on learning she was pregnant. That she retained a belief in the essential goodness of mankind seemed to him a sign of either saintliness or stupidity.

'What is it, Gavin?' Lucy asked.

Even over the line, the note of worry in her voice had been obvious. 'I thought I'd just let you know I've been asked to go to the police station.'

'Why?'

'They want to question me again.'

'But you can't tell them anything more. It must mean they don't believe you.'

'Not necessarily. George thinks it may well be a bit of a bluff on their part.'

'George who?'

'Waite.'

'You've seen him? Gavin, don't treat me as if I'd collapse at the first breath of bad news. You're afraid things are becoming really difficult, aren't you?'

'Perhaps a little.'

'What does George say?'

'It's just possible they may . . . well, arrest me. But he hopes it won't come to that and he'll be able to persuade them that what I've been telling them is the truth.'

There was a long silence before she said, 'Does he think he'll be able to do that?'

'He's reasonably confident.'

'When are you going to the police station?'

'As soon as I ring off.'

'Good luck, my darling.'

She rang off before he said goodbye. She would, he was certain, now swallow a couple of the homeopathic calming tablets in which she had great faith. A friend had once said to him that Lucy was obviously capable of coping with anything without even becoming fussed. That erroneous judgement showed how well she hid her nervous character.

He left the room and made his way down the stairs.

The desk sergeant asked their names and Waite gave them and the reason for their visit. He spoke briefly over the internal phone. 'DI Ingham says he'll be with you as soon as he's free and will you be kind enough to wait until then.'

They crossed to a bench seat, the cover of which was stained and at one point torn. A drunk, propelled by two uniformed policemen, was brought in; he incoherently answered the desk sergeant's questions, had the contents of his pockets put into a plastic bag and was helped through to the cells. A woman, accompanied by a WPC, cursed the WPC and the desk sergeant in the crudest terms as her arrest was booked; she was taken to the cells. A man, asked to empty his pockets, suddenly lost all sense of reason and began to attack his escort; a fellow PC rushed to assist and a brief, vicious fight left one PC limping and the arrested man bloody and dazed . . .

'Let's get the hell out of here,' Penfold said, as he stood.

'It will be better—' Waite began.

'If he can't be bothered to speak to me, I'm damned if I can see why I should stay.'

'To have to see how the other half lives? It is a disagreeable eye-opener, but frankly it would be a mistake to leave now. The inspector is probably deliberately waiting to question you to try to get your nerves jangling.'

'I thought you said he was straightforward?'

'Unnerving a witness is straightforward police policy, much favoured because its use can seldom be proved.'

Penfold sat.

A woman whose dress branded her a prostitute offered the custody sergeant her personal well-tried services if he would agree to drop the charge; when he declined both to do that and the pleasure of her services, she cursed him in terms that surprised even him. A rabbit of a man, accused of kerb-crawling, began to sob as he finally accepted that his wife must learn what he had been doing. A youngster, high on drugs, was searched and a small amount of what appeared to be crack was found; he was escorted to an interview room to be held there until a close relative could be present when he was questioned. A drunken woman, wearing a dressing gown over underclothes, claimed it was someone she knew only by sight who had insisted on playing the music centre at full volume and then assaulted the man from the next flat who had complained; she had never kicked anyone and most certainly not the complainant as he lay on the floor . . .

Young walked up to where they sat. 'Would you come this way?'

They followed him down a corridor, through the charge room, and into the first of the three interview rooms. This was square and bleak, the only furniture a table, on which was a tape recorder, four chairs and a framed list of witness's rights. They sat on the left of the table, Young on the right.

A moment later Ingham entered, greeted them, thanked them for coming to the station and sat. 'Shall we begin?' He nodded at Young, who switched on the tape recorder and said, 'The time is fifteen-o-six on the sixteenth of November. Present are Mr Penfold, here voluntarily, Mr Waite, DC Young, and DI Ingham.'

Ingham began the questioning. 'I am making enquiries into an incident which occurred in the village of Oak Cross on the eighth of November at approximately nineteen thirty-five, in which Mrs Muriel Lynch was knocked down and seriously injured by a car that failed to stop. There is reason to believe that the car in question was a Jaguar, belonging to you, Mr Penfold. Was it your car?'

'For God's sake . . .' he began heatedly. His leg was nudged by Waite's. He said more calmly, 'I do not know for certain whether or not it was my car.'

'Why is that?'

'Because after I drove from Hallam House and was on my way home, I was boxed in by two cars . . .' It was the truth, but in that bleak room, it seemed even to him that he was telling a story of impossible colours . . .

The questioning ended at a quarter past seven when Ingham said, 'Gavin Penfold, I am arresting you for having driven when under the influence of alcohol on the eighth of this month, contrary to section 5(1)a of the Road Traffic Act 1988 and schedule 2 of the Road Offenders Act 1988; for injuring a pedestrian, Mrs Muriel Lynch, and for not stopping after the accident, contrary to section 174 of the Road Traffic Act 1988 and schedule 2 of the Road Offenders Act 1988. You do not have to say anything, but it may harm your defence if you do not mention something you later rely on in court. Whatever you do say may be used in evidence. Do you understand that?'

'I was not driving my Jaguar because I was bound, gagged, blindfolded and jammed down in the back well. I do not know who was driving when it hit Mrs Lynch other than that his name was Al.'

'Interview terminated at seventeen fifteen hours.'

The tape recorder was switched off.

'You will, of course, allow my client bail until he appears before the magistrates?' Waite said.

'It is a serious offence,' Ingham answered.

'My client has from the beginning of your investigation denied any culpability and therefore he is eager to prove his innocence. He is hardly likely to endanger his chance of doing this by trying to avoid appearing in court when his presence is demanded. Further, the crimes of which he is accused do not in any way suggest he might be a danger to anyone else if he maintains his freedom.'

'Very well,' Ingham said.

Penfold drove the Astra into the left-hand bay of the garage. As he walked towards the house, both illuminated and cast into shadow by the outside lights, he found himself regarding it with the sad bitterness of seeing something he valued in danger of being lost.

'What happened?' Lucy demanded as he opened the outside door.

He stepped inside, closed the door. 'I've been charged.'

'Christ!'

He hugged her, giving and seeking inner strength.

'Why didn't George stop them?' she demanded wildly, voice slightly muffled because her mouth was partially against him.

'He couldn't make them understand I was telling the truth. The best he managed was to persuade them to release me on bail.'

'What . . . what happens now?'

'There'll be a hearing before magistrates, who'll decide whether or not I should go on trial.'

'But George will stop them doing that?'

'He'll have counsel representing me.'

'Whoever it is, George is sure they'll be persuaded you can't be tried for something you didn't do?'

A lie would comfort her, but that comfort would probably

be short-lived. 'Let's go into the sitting room and have a drink.'

'Tell me what George thinks?'

'It could be tricky.'

'You may be tried?'

'Yes.'

'The bloody fools,' she shouted.

She swore so seldom it was as if she had used up the whole vocabulary of four-letter words. He released her and stepped back. 'Come on, my love, let's go through. Things are never so bad after a Martini and tonic.'

That night, it was she who initiated sex. Normally quietly passionate, she became so wild it was as if he were in bed with a stranger. Afterwards they lay side by side, their fears temporarily banished by their love.

Thirteen

Myers looked across the CID general room. 'Never been told you don't get paid for looking into space?'

Kendrick jerked his mind away from the pressing question, Had he and Margaret argued so much yesterday evening that she'd really meant it when she'd said that perhaps they shouldn't see each other for a day or two? 'I was thinking.'

'Makes a change . . . Heard the news?'

'Depends what news.'

'The guv'nor had the papers back from the CPS with a green light, so he hauled Penfold in for questioning and then charged him.'

Because his life had become cloudy, Kendrick spoke rashly. 'And now you're happy.'

'Dead right. I am happy to see the drunken bastard who ran down an old girl end up in court. And if you're asking, I'll be even happier if he goes down for a good stretch.'

'And your happiness will be complete when you imagine him in a cell instead of that lovely old manor house.'

'You're beginning to annoy me.'

'So you'll write in your report that I'm poor material, not up to CID standards, and you'll buy yourself a bottle of champagne the day I'm back in uniform.'

'There's no call to talk like that.'

'I don't reckon it's great to see him kicked in the nuts just because he's a sight better off than we'll ever be.'

'You're talking daft. It's not like that.'

'No?'

'You youngsters haven't even got sparrow brains. I'm thinking of the victim.'

'Can you even remember her name?'

'If you're trying to cause trouble . . .' He stopped as Ingham entered.

'I need a draft evidence file on the Penfold case by lunch time.'

'That could be a bit optimistic . . .' Myers began.

'If I want optimism, I don't come to you. Lunch time, on my desk.' He left.

'It's easy to ask the impossible when it's not you having to do it,' Myers said, his previous annoyance overtaken by present resentment.

'I suppose it's likely Mr Penfold will be up before the magistrates tomorrow.'

'On a Saturday?'

'I'd forgotten.'

'Catch them working on a Saturday and you'll see blue moons.'

'I've read that there are conditions when the moon does appear to be blue. Atmospheric conditions, I suppose.'

'Too many pints, more like . . . Come on, then, start slaving or we'll have the guv'nor shouting his head off.'

Penfold and Waite had to wait in chambers for only a couple of minutes before the chief clerk showed them into Hindhead's room.

'Morning, George . . . Good morning, Mr Penfold.' Hindhead half-turned to face his companion. 'I don't think you know Reg Smythe who'll be my junior.'

They shook hands; Penfold and Waite sat in front of the desk, Smythe to one side, Hindhead behind it.

Hindhead, QC, was a man of medium height and medium build who possessed the ability to appear to be of no more than medium competence – a deception never more valuable than in the criminal courts. With his round head topped by a somewhat moth-eaten wig – suggesting the financial inability to afford a new one – a round, pudgy face in which brown eyes often appeared to project puzzlement, a button of a nose and a broad smiling face, he presented a Pickwickian air. When he was prosecuting for the Crown, criminals who assumed him to be an easy mark because of his appearance and manner sooner or later learned their mistake.

'You have received the last batch of papers?' Waite asked.

'A courier delivered them soon after you rang to say they were on their way.' Hindhead opened the folder on his desk. 'I think I should say at the beginning that this is not going to be an easy case to win.' His mellow voice was redolent of port and cigars. 'I'm sure, Mr Penfold, that you appreciate that?'

'I'm not certain I do. I cannot understand how, when I've told the truth from the beginning, the police refuse to accept that is what it is, and I'm now to be tried for a crime I did not commit.'

'The police are conditioned to the normal routine of crime and so find considerable difficulty in accepting the unusual. One has to admit that the facts of this case are unusual.' He picked up a sheet of paper from the folder, briefly read, then put it down. 'Although I will, of course, propose to the magistrates that there is no case to answer, we should accept that they will reject that and will send you to trial. So I propose to treat this conference as being more relevant to the trial than the hearing . . . Would you agree with that, George?'

'Yes,' Waite said.

'Mr Penfold, in order to establish the credibility of all your evidence, we have to be able to offer a credible motive for your kidnapping, enforced drunkenness, and abandonment in your car at your home. Obviously, the two incidents are not necessarily connected – indeed, it is in your interests that they most certainly were not. Your kidnapping was planned, making you drunk a necessity which arose after Mrs Lynch was knocked down and injured by your car . . . You have suggested the motive for the kidnapping must be to do with your employment at the Counties Bank, but cannot provide a specific link. Is that still so?'

'I have access to every corner of the bank's IT systems. I imagine they hoped to force me to transfer money electronically to an offshore bank from which authority would not be able to recover it.'

'You have reason for suggesting this?'

'No more than comes from being unable to suggest anything else.'

'And you'd hold that they did not proceed with this plan because the driver of your car was driving so recklessly he hit Mrs Lynch and severely injured her; they feared the police might be able to trace the car very quickly and would be looking to question you, which would make it too dangerous to continue with their plan. So, in order to cover their tracks as far as possible, they set the scene in such a way that the police would refuse to believe what you told them. Is that how you interpret events?'

'Yes.'

'Was it ever suggested you might become an accomplice to an electronic theft?'

'You think I wouldn't have reported it?' Penfold asked angrily.

'I am sure you would, but I am afraid these questions have to be asked by me, however much they offend, because they will probably be asked by the prosecution.'

'I . . . I'm sorry.'

'A perfectly understandable reaction. If there has never been a direct approach, could there in the past have been an indirect one which you failed to recognize as such then, but now can identify?'

'I don't think, if there had been, I would have failed to identify it, however indirect. One becomes paranoid about security . . .'

An hour and twenty minutes later, there was a short break during which they drank tea or coffee and ate chocolate biscuits. After the under-clerk had collected the tray, the consultation continued.

'There is an important point which needs to be covered,' Hindhead said. 'Are you a heavy drinker?'

'I am not,' Penfold answered.

'Have you ever suffered from alcohol problems?'

'I didn't drink voluntarily; I was forced to do so. I don't even like whisky.'

'What I'm asking is: do you have a history of heavy drinking?'

'How heavy is heavy?'

'Very difficult to be precise, of course, because in the context it will be the jury who determine the standard. To put things at their starkest: recently, have friends seen you the worse for drink? You realize why I'm asking?'

'No.'

'The prosecution will seek to show that when you consumed so much alcohol that Friday night, it was of your own free will. A history of heavy drinking will buttress such an assertion. Therefore, if they have gained such evidence, the court might be persuaded to allow it to be introduced and as a consequence we have to be ready to rebut it.'

Penfold spoke with bitter reluctance. 'There was a time when the stress of work became so great that I started to drink quite heavily. When I realized this, I pulled myself together.'

'Did you ever drink heavily in circumstances which might come to light?'

'Several of our friends are pretty heavy social drinkers, so I can't think I stood out.'

'But one or more might testify that you did at times drink heavily?'

'If they're friends?'

'Some friends are best compared to weathercocks, turning with the wind. Let's hope either yours are made of finer material or the prosecution can find no allowable reason to produce such evidence in court. One final question: there was no incident which could have drawn the attention of someone perhaps less reluctant to repeat it than one hopes a friend would be?'

'No. Unless . . .'

'You have remembered something?'

'We had lunch with my in-laws and . . . The stress of work had become fierce and I did drink more than usual – in fact, so much that I all but passed out at the end of the meal. My wife had difficulty in getting me into our car. Later she said . . . said the most humiliating aspect was that the gardener saw me.'

'Then we have to be prepared for the incident to be known to the prosecution and for them to try to introduce the details in court.' Hindhead massaged his round chin with thumb and forefinger. 'Do you remember whether you were at that time suffering from an ailment which necessitated medicine that might well have exacerbated the effects of alcohol?'

'No, I don't.'

'It might well be worth discussing the matter with your wife; her memory could be firmer than yours.'

Why didn't he name a medicine that would be accepted as relevant? Or did legal ethics forbid his actually providing an accused with a defence? Penfold bitterly wondered.

The hearing before magistrates took place on the 22nd and 23rd. The prosecution presented their case, there was very little cross-examination, and the defence was reserved.

Penfold was committed to appear at the Crown Court; bail was renewed.

On Thursday, while Lucy prepared breakfast, Penfold went out to the small and ancient dog kennel in which the newspapers were left each morning. Being a Friday, in addition to *The Times*, there was a copy of the *Pettersgrove Gazette*, a weekly newspaper almost as parochial as its name suggested, which owed its profitable circulation to a policy of reporting every village event, naming as many names as possible. Personalities, not news, sold local newspapers.

He opened the *Gazette*, struggling to hold the pages in the wind, and read the legal reports. Because a local builder had appeared on a charge of criminally incompetent work, resulting in a woman's death, his own appearance before the local magistrates had rated only eight single-column lines.

As he entered the kitchen, Lucy looked up. 'Is there anything?'

'A brief report.'

'What's it say? Does it mention you by name?'

Had she been hoping for the cloak of anonymity? Then she had forgotten that justice had not only to be done, it had to be seen to be done, even if initial publicity might result in the injustice of the accused's being deemed guilty before the trial by a public whose prurient interest seldom lay in innocence.

'Can't you answer? What does it say?'

He handed her the paper. 'Right-hand side, at the bottom.'

The toaster popped up. He put down *The Times*, picked out the two slices of toast and put them in the toast rack, inserted two more slices of bread.

She lowered the paper. 'There's hardly anything, thank God!'

She was obviously hoping that what had been printed would not be read by anyone they knew.

'Did Hindhead tell the magistrates how prejudiced the police are being?'

'He hardly cross-examined.'

'Why not?'

'I gather it's a question of tactics. The less the defence says in a magistrates' court, the less able the prosecution is to judge what exact line the defence will take at the trial.'

The toaster popped up again and he put the toast in the

110

rack. 'Now that everything's out in the open, we ought to tell your parents what's happening so that they're prepared.'

'I did that some time ago.'

He opened a cupboard, brought out a tray and put the toast rack on it. 'How did they react?'

'Mother said that if there's anything they can do to help, we just have to ask.'

'That's more than generous of them in view of the past; they must wonder if perhaps I was drunk and hit—'

'They will not think any such thing because I explained what really happened. They know you've told the police the truth over and over again, but they just won't listen. Mother said that when the case gets thrown out of court, she'll put up two fingers at the first policeman she meets and make father buy a case of her favourite champagne, which we'll all drink.'

He managed to smile. 'You've wonderful parents.'

'And a wonderful husband.' She kissed him. 'The coffee machine's bubbling, so will you take it off the stove while I try to find the raspberry jam you like so much – I bought another two jars, but for the moment simply can't remember where I put them.'

Engels crossed to Penfold's work station just after three thirty, Friday afternoon. 'Have you time for a word, Gavin?'

'Here and now?'

'Yes, but better upstairs.'

'Then I'll be with you as soon as I've cemented.'

'Fine.'

Engels left. The head of human resources was friendly, broad-minded, and devious – he would always drop someone else in the cess-pit if that enabled him to remain sparkling clean.

Penfold closed down the work he was doing, after double-checking that he had stored it, and made his way up to the small office on the next floor. 'Is there a problem?' he asked, once seated.

'In a sense.'

'So what is it?'

Engels scratched the side of his neck, shifted in the chair, rearranged some papers on the desk. 'I was called to Mr Seagor's office earlier.'

'Did you remember to bow on entering?'

'Talking like that hardly promotes team spirit, you know.'

'But it helps promote the suspicion that he really does believe he can walk on water.'

'He showed me this week's copy of the *Pettersgrove Gazette*.'

Abruptly Penfold understood why he'd been asked up to the other's office and that his snide remarks were about to be repaid with interest.

'Mr Seagor read about the drunken driver who knocked down and injured a woman and whose name was Gavin Penfold. He said he found it impossible to believe you were the Gavin Penfold mentioned.'

'I'm grateful for his trust.'

'Nevertheless, he would be grateful if you would confirm it was not you.'

'I seem to have expressed my gratitude too soon.'

'Do you confirm that?'

'I was not driving the Jaguar that knocked Mrs Lynch down.'

'But it was your car?'

'So the police claim.'

'But you weren't in it?'

'On the contrary. But I wasn't driving, because I was stuffed like a trussed chicken into the back well.'

Engels said, looking at a space above Penfold's head, 'That's a strange story.'

'How else does one describe a strange experience?'

Engels cleared his throat. 'Since you have been sent for

trial, one has to imagine that the police do not believe you.'

'A policeman is trained to disbelieve.'

'They must be very certain you were driving.'

'The circumstances were such that it was far easier for them to come to the obvious and incorrect conclusion.'

'You must appreciate this makes things very difficult.'

'My understanding in that respect began when the police first showed they disbelieved me.'

'I'm referring to the bank.'

'I can't say I've thought about that aspect of things – been far too concerned with my own problems.'

'I – Mr Seagor – have every confidence that you will be completely cleared at your trial.'

'There's nothing so heartening as expressions of genuine trust.'

'But you will understand that the bank has to take a very wide attitude.'

'If I knew what that really meant, I might well agree.'

'It has to be exceedingly damaging to the image of a bank of our standing to have a senior security employee charged with a crime.'

'I'd have thought that depended on the image and the crime.'

'I'm sorry you're taking this attitude.'

'My stiff back makes it difficult to genuflect.'

'Mr Seagor says . . . You must understand it is not my decision to make.'

'But it's not one from which you dissent?'

'Until the matter is cleared up satisfactorily, it will be best if you're suspended from work.'

'Guilty until proven innocent?'

'Suspended on full pay, of course.'

'Hedging the bets, as always?'

Fourteen

January, ever a perverse month, brought dry and sunny weather; one journalistic Jeremiah even prognosticated drought conditions in the summer. As the judge entered and the court stood, a shaft of sunlight came through a round window and highlighted the painting on the opposite wall whose presence was as controversial as the identity of the man in full wig – why had it hung there for decades, contrary to courtroom protocol, and who was the subject?

Mr Justice Brown sat and the court settled. He rearranged the notebook and three different-coloured ball-point pens his clerk had put on the desk, ignored the small VDU and looked across the well of the court at prosecuting counsel with concealed disapproval. Christine Ryan – in her late forties, tall, dark-haired, dressed with smart conservatism – could, unlike so many female barristers and judges, wear gown, tabs and a wig without looking faintly risible, but the law had been ordained to be within men's domain because its unbiased administration called for clear, logical thought.

'Regina versus Gavin John Penfold,' said the clerk, his voice pitched surprisingly high for a man of his considerable bulk.

Christine Ryan rose, gave her gown a tug, flicked the tails of her wig clear of her collar. 'Members of the jury, this case concerns events which took place on the sixteenth of November of last year in the village of Oak Cross. At around seven thirty in the evening, Mrs Lynch was returning home and had occasion to cross the road which runs through the centre of the village. I should point out that there is some doubt as to the correct name for this road . . .'

Women so often concentrated on inconsequential matters, the judge thought . . .

Hindhead stood. 'Mrs Gill, you have given your evidence with great clarity, so there are only one or two questions I need to ask.'

In no way misled by this polite praise, she stared at him with sharp suspicion.

'You have said the car came round the corner much too quickly. What speed do you judge it was doing?'

'I can't say.'

'You would not like to make an estimate?'

'I would not.'

'Yet presumably you have some standard, some base reference, which provokes you to state it was going too quickly?'

'Yes.'

'Will you tell the court what that is?'

'I've lived in Oak Cross for the past twenty years and have seen hundreds of vehicles come round the corner. Most of them do so slowly because it is so sharp. The Jaguar was travelling more quickly than any other I remember; so quickly the tyres were squealing.'

'Do you know what makes a car tyre squeal?'

'Speed.'

'Not necessarily, Mrs Gill. Road surface, tyre condition and pressure, angle of turn . . .'

'Mr Hindhead,' said the judge, 'are we to take it that you put yourself forward as an expert as to the cause of tyre squeal?'

'No, my Lord, merely—'

'Then should you wish to draw a conclusion you ask the court to accept, it might be better if you called such an expert.'

'My Lord, all I am trying to establish is that it would be a mistake to accept the sound of tyre squeal as irrefutable evidence of excessive speed.'

'Merely of motion.'

There was brief laughter, which annoyed the judge because he had not been trying to be amusing. Humour was the province of humorists, not judges.

'As the car drove away after Mrs Lynch was knocked to the ground, you had the presence of mind to try to read the registration number. You succeeded in doing so except in respect of the last letter, and this was because you were not wearing your distance glasses. Is that correct?'

'Yes.'

'And later you told the police what you had seen and identified the car as a Jaguar. Can you identify many different makes of cars?'

'As I said earlier, an acquaintance owns a Jaguar and the car I saw that night was exactly similar.'

'Presumably you did not take much notice of it until after the collision with Mrs Lynch?'

'I noticed it when I heard the tyres squeal as it came round the corner so quickly.'

'At that point, you had no pressing reason to identify its make, did you?'

She hesitated. 'Not really, no.'

'Your sharp interest was only aroused after you saw it hit Mrs Lynch?'

'Yes.'

'And by then it was going away from you and you could only study the back of it?'

'I knew it was a Jaguar.'

'Very well.' His cross-examination had gained nothing and had not been intended to do so, because there could be no doubt that the car had been the defendant's; his aim had been to establish in the jury's minds the feeling that the witness was too sure of herself. 'What did you do after Mrs Lynch was hit by the car?'

'I hurried to see if I could help her and ring for an ambulance.'

'You did not immediately rush to where she lay, did you?'

'Of course I did.'

'Yet you've told us you did your best to read the registration number of the departing car.'

'That took very little time.'

'Even though you had trouble reading the number? That surely means that for a while you were watching the car?'

'I suppose so. But as I've just said, it was only for a few seconds.'

'Yet long enough to note also how the car was being driven?'

'Even more quickly,' she said aggressively.

'Was it weaving from side to side of the road as it drove off?'

'No.'

'Then it was travelling in a controlled manner?'

'Yes.'

'You are quite certain of that?'

'Yes.'

'You told the police that as it drove away, you chanced to look up at the rear window and thought you saw a shape. Is that the precise description you originally gave?'

'No.'

Hindhead looked down at his papers, paused long enough to create a slight impression of expectancy, then looked up once more. 'What exactly did you tell the officer? Please try to remember your exact words.'

'I said I thought I saw a face looking through the rear window.'

'You thought you saw a face looking through the rear window.' Hindhead repeated the words slowly and portentously as he faced the jury and wondered how many of them would possess sufficient intelligence and interest in the proceedings to understand the significance of this. 'Would you tell the court why you have changed your description from face to shape?'

'The police pointed out that the car was quite a long way away by then and I wasn't wearing my distance glasses.'

'And did they also point out that since you'd been unable to read the last letter of the registration number, your ability to distinguish detail at an increasing distance had to be poor?'

'I think they said something like that.'

'They were building up in your mind the thought you could not be certain what you had seen.'

The judge intervened. 'Mrs Gill, will you tell us again whether it was before or after you read the registration number that you saw the face or shape?'

'I tried very hard to read the last letter, but of course it became more and more indistinct, so I looked up and saw . . .' She did not finish.

'Something,' supplied Hindhead, before the judge could speak, 'which you originally took to be a face, and it was only after the police had questioned you at considerable length, perhaps adding that many car owners have dangling animals in their back windows, that you changed your description from face to shape?'

'Yes.'

'Yet we have heard that no toy was found dangling in front of the rear window of the Jaguar.' Hindhead sat.

Christine Ryan stood. 'Mrs Gill, would you say you can make up your own mind?'

'I certainly would,' she answered firmly and with a touch of annoyance that there should be any doubt.

'You are not swayed this way and that by other people's opinions or suggestions?'

'Certainly not.'

'However much someone tried to persuade you to change

your mind, you would resist such pressure if you thought it right to do so?'

'Of course.'

'As we have heard, the police did point out that the car must have been a fair way away by the time you looked at the rear window and also that car owners often have toy animals on elastic or string above the back shelves of their cars. Did you believe they were trying to make you alter what you had originally said?'

'I don't think I did, no.'

'But you did change your description from face to shape.'

'I realized I could not say beyond any doubt that what I had seen was a face.'

'We must be quite clear about this. Was your doubt fostered solely by the police?'

'By what they said, yes. But had I decided they could not be right, I would have ignored their words.'

'Thank you, Mrs Gill. That is all.' Christine Ryan sat.

Hindhead turned and spoke to Smythe as the witness left the box. 'Hopefully, we can call that deuce.'

'You did get her to say the car was driven steadily after the accident, which suggests it wasn't a drunken driver at the wheel.'

'But how firmly, when the men in the jury, and possibly the women as well, think back to the times they've driven when half seas over and been convinced they were as steady as ever?'

Myers despised lawyers – hated and despised defence lawyers. They knowingly used their skills to promote the unjust verdicts that enabled villains to escape the consequences of their crimes; yet, try as he might, he could not prevent himself acknowledging their authority almost with servility. 'We drove into the yard of Alten Cobb at about nine-thirty, sir.'

'But as we have learned –' Hindhead turned his head so that the jury could clearly see his expression of mannered surprise – 'you did not go immediately to the house and announce yourselves and the reason for your presence, but examined the car which was outside the garage. That was a very incorrect procedure, was it not?'

'I don't think so, sir.'

'That an unheralded invasion of someone's property may well engender fear in the minds of the occupants is of no account?'

'But—'

'The police do not stop to consider that their actions may well arouse fear in others?'

'Of course they do.'

'Then you are an exception?'

'No. What—'

'You had a strange way of showing your concern. You acted in a manner which forced Mrs Penfold, one may say bravely, to leave the safety of her home before she could learn who you were and that you were not intending a violent burglary.'

'It was important to examine the Jaguar before the evidence could be tampered with.'

'Who might have been the tamperer?'

'Someone who lived in the house.'

'You believed that on a dark, unpleasant November evening, someone in the house was about to tamper with evidence when they could have done so long before your arrival?'

'What I'm trying to say—'

'It would help if you could give evidence that needs no explanation.'

'Perhaps,' the judge said, 'the witness would find that easier if he were allowed to give it.'

'Much obliged, Your Lordship,' Hindhead said aloud. Bloody old fool, he said under his breath. He leaned forward and spoke briefly to Waite, in the final row of seats. He straightened up. 'Having examined the Jaguar, what did you do?'

'Went to the house and asked to speak to Mr Penfold.'

'Asked?'

'Yes, sir.'

'Mrs Penfold will describe your attitude as overbearing and threatening.'

'I am sure my colleague will confirm that it was not.'

'Mrs Penfold did not refuse to allow you to see Mr Penfold, did she?'

'She said he was too ill.'

'Quite. But that was a good reason, not a refusal. Yet having been told he was ill, you still said that if she did not allow you to speak to him, you would enforce your will.'

'I needed to see him.'

'Why?'

'To judge whether he was under the influence of alcohol.'

'You were convinced he was drunk even before you had seen him, let alone spoken to him?'

'The evidence inside the car led me to that belief.'

'What evidence?'

'The vomit and the empty bottle.'

'Vomit is a frequent evidence of illness, is it not?'

'Yes, sir.'

'But you were pleased automatically to assume it to be evidence of drunkenness?'

'It seemed probable in view of the empty whisky bottle.'

'Which for all you knew had been in the car for many days?'

'There was a smell of whisky.'

'Discernible above the far stronger and no doubt obnoxious smell of vomit? I suggest you assumed there must be a smell of whisky rather than that you actually discerned it.'

'No.'

'Had you determined whether Mr Penfold enjoyed drinking whisky?'

'No, sir.'

'Had you done so, you would have learned that he dislikes

whisky and never voluntarily drinks it . . . The defence does not question the fact that when you saw Mr Penfold, he was suffering from the ingestion of a very considerable amount of whisky, yet far from this having been voluntarily, it had been against his will. Yet your answers to my questions show that even before you entered the house you were convinced Mr Penfold had been driving the Jaguar after voluntarily drinking so heavily that he had knocked down Mrs Lynch and not stopped.'

Myers, despite his resentment, had been too often in the witness box to lose his temper when once more being called a liar or a bigot or both. 'I was certain of nothing before I entered the house. I was collecting such evidence as was available so that later it could be evaluated.'

'Then let us see how far this fair-minded attitude which you claim stretched. Once in the house, did you not demand to see Mr Penfold and threaten Mrs Penfold if she did not comply with your demand?'

'I told her I had to see her husband and would like her permission to do so. I added that if she insisted on refusing my request, I would have to obtain the necessary legal powers.'

'There are many ways of expressing the law's wishes. Mrs Penfold felt very threatened by the method you chose.'

'She would say that, wouldn't she?'

'What are you inferring?' Hindhead demanded sharply.

'Mr Hindhead,' the judge said, 'I doubt the officer was wishing to infer anything.'

'Then with respect, My Lord, he has an unusual way of expressing that negative . . . Constable, you were shown into a bedroom and on the bed lay Mr Penfold. Describe his condition.'

'He was naked. He was breathing heavily and noisily; his complexion was pallid. By the side of the bed was a bucket and there was vomit in it.'

'Did you speak to him?'

'I tried to, but it was a waste of time.'

'Why was that?'

'He was completely drunk.'

'You are an expert on intoxication?'

'Experience has taught me when someone is too far gone to be able to get any sense out of him.'

'In other words, you judged him, in common parlance, to be completely under the table?'

'Yes, sir.'

'A judgement endorsed by medical examination. Tell me: with your considerable experience in drunkenness, would you say that a man in such condition as was my client, would be capable of driving at all, let alone from Oak Cross to his home in Fieldhurst?'

'On the face of things, it might seem unlikely, but I have seen a man drive a car when I wouldn't have thought he could find the steering wheel.'

'Drive in a careful, controlled manner or an incompetent one? Surely one has merely to note the manner in which the vehicle is being driven to know the driver to be under the influence?'

'Most times, yes, sir.'

'We have heard evidence that after the Jaguar had hit and injured Mrs Lynch, it was driven away very quickly and in a perfectly controlled manner. There are two explanations how this could be, are there not?'

Myers did not answer.

'One, the driver was so drunk that later he was described as being almost in a coma, yet contrary to common sense was able to drive in a normal, safe, controlled manner; two, that the driver was not drunk. Would you agree?'

'Yes, but . . .'

'Well?'

'Nothing, sir.'

'Do you still believe Mr Penfold could have been the driver of his car when it struck Mrs Lynch?'

Before Myers could answer, the judge said, 'Constable, you said you have experience of observing people who have consumed a great deal of alcohol yet are capable of driving a car?'

'Yes, My Lord.'

'Was it their driving which led to their being stopped and questioned?'

'Not every time, My Lord.'

'Can you give the court an example when it was not, which comes from personal experience?'

'Before I was in CID, I was in Traffic. One night we were passed by a car with a rear light out and we stopped him. He smelled of liquor. So we breathalysed him and he was almost off the scale.'

'He was inebriated?'

'As drunk as a . . . Very drunk, My Lord.'

'Before you stopped the car, had the manner of his driving led you to suspect he might be under the influence of alcohol?'

'No, My Lord.'

'Thank you.' The judge wrote in his notebook.

'Constable,' Hindhead said, 'did you arrest the driver and take him to the police station where he was charged?'

'Yes, sir.'

'What happened then?'

'He was released on police bail.'

'He left the station?'

'Yes, sir.'

'He was drunk within legal terms, but in fact far from about to lapse into semi-consciousness or even a coma . . . Thank you.' Hindhead sat. He turned round and spoke to Smythe: 'We've got a judge who thinks he's appearing for the prosecution.'

Lucy had found the magistrates' hearing so emotionally distressing she had decided not to attend the trial unless her husband asked her to; she had been grateful he had suggested it would be much better if she stayed at home. But by the time he returned in the evening, she did not know which was the worse: to *know* what was happening, or to dread what *might* be happening.

As he entered the hall, she said, tension making her sound breathless, 'How did it go? Are they optimistic?'

He linked his arm with hers. 'Hindhead made some telling points, but as he said yet again, I have to convince the jury when I give my evidence.'

'Which you will. I know you will. And then this awful time will be over.'

Fifteen

It was midday Wednesday.

'Do you work in the Finger-print Section of the Home Office Forensic laboratory at Stetchford?' Christine Ryan asked.

'I do.' Ritchie was tall and thin; his sallow face was scarred from childhood acne.

'And were a bottle and bottle cap, exhibits fourteen and fifteen – now being handed to you – sent to you to be examined?'

He looked at the items, in plastic bags. 'They were.'

'What were your findings regarding these two items?'

'The cap is ridged around the side and it is very difficult to record prints of any value on it; there were none on the top. On the bottle there was one clear set of prints which, using comparison prints, I identified as those of Mr Penfold.'

Christine Ryan sat; Hindhead stood.

'You found only one set of prints on the bottle?'

'That is correct.'

'Did this seem surprising?'

'To a degree.'

'Because a bottle bought in a supermarket will have been handled by a number of persons and you would expect to find more than one set of prints or other individual prints?'

'Yes.'

'Can you offer an explanation for this apparent lack of a variety of prints?'

'In my opinion, the bottle had been wiped down.'

'What leads you to that conclusion?'

'The lack of other impressions and the kind of appearance one finds on glass if the material used to wipe it is not very clean.'

'You are saying it had been wiped down prior to the impression of the prints you found?'

'I'm saying it probably had been.'

'Are the prints clear?'

'Very clear.'

'Would you expect prints recorded inadvertently – by which I mean, when a bottle is casually picked up – to be so clear?'

'It can obviously happen.'

'But not frequently?'

'I think it's impossible to answer that.'

'If prints are deliberately recorded – for instance to inculpate an innocent man – one would expect them to be very clear?'

'I'm sorry, but once again, I don't think I can answer.'

'Perhaps one can suggest that they would only be so very clear if the unwitting donor were semi-conscious or unconscious.' Hindhead sat.

Abacassis took the oath.

'You are an assistant at the Home Office Forensic laboratory at Stitchford?' Christine Ryan asked.

'Yes.' A man of casual habits, his attempt to tidy his appearance had been a failure.

'Were the empty litre bottle of Famous Grouse whisky, exhibit fourteen, and the cap, exhibit fifteen, sent to you for examination and did you examine them?'

'I did.'

'Please tell the court your findings.'

'Under magnification, it was possible to compare the edges of the metal left around the neck of the bottle with the cap. I was able to judge that the cap came from that bottle.'

'Is there room for any doubt?'

'I do not think so.'

'No questions,' Hindhead said, without bothering to rise.

Cameron's examination-in-chief was completed early on Wednesday afternoon. To those with courtroom experience, his attitude spoke of witness-nervousness.

Hindhead rose, leaned forward and spoke to Waite, turned and leaned over to speak to Smythe.

'Are you intending to question the witness?' demanded the judge, quickly annoyed by any delay not of his own causing.

Hindhead faced the witness box. 'Mr Cameron, at the end of a working day, employees often leave in groups of four, five, six, maybe more, as they discuss the past, present, or future. Does that in your experience happen at Hallam House?'

'Yes.'

'At such moments, there can be little chance of identifying every person in the group?'

'If it's a real crowd, no chance.'

'If such a group leaves the building after you have come on duty at six, you will be unable to identify each person who has left?'

'I've just said.'

'Did such a group leave Hallam House after six on Friday, the eighth of November last year?'

'I can't rightly remember.'

'You do not enjoy a good memory?'

'It's a long time ago.'

'And time draws a veil over memory?'

'Mr Hindhead,' the judge said, 'I think we may accept that it can be difficult accurately to remember a specific detail on a day some months ago.'

'My Lord, I am much obliged for your pointing out that since the witness cannot say who left Hallam House before

128

seven that Friday, he cannot say my client did.' Hindhead addressed the witness once more. 'Having established that, we will now examine what happened after seven. Where were you at that time?'

'At the control desk, where I was meant to be.'

'And during the following fifteen minutes?'

'I stayed there like my orders say.'

'We have heard evidence which proves my client did not leave the building by any of the emergency exits. Consequently, it must have been by the main entrance. The log book which you are obliged to keep shows you did not leave the control desk after your six o'clock round and before your nine o'clock round. Are your entries for that night correct?'

'Yes.'

'Then if my client left just after seven, you would have seen and identified him?'

'Yes.'

'And he would have seen you?'

'Yes.'

'But he did not see you because you were not at the control desk.'

'Yes, I was.'

'I put it to you, you are lying.'

'The log shows I was at the desk.'

'It shows you made no entry to record that you temporarily left your post at around seven that evening.'

'If I had, I'd have written it down.'

'Would you?'

'Yes.'

'You never leave your post without recording that fact?'

'No.'

'If you had reason to be away from it and out of sight of the entrance for only the briefest time, during which there was no reason to think anything untoward had happened, you would still note your absence?'

'Yes.'

'You wouldn't consider that to be observing the letter of the regulations to an excessive degree and beyond what was intended?'

'No.'

'You don't think most people would regard a momentary absence as of insufficient consequence to be recorded?'

'Can't say.'

'I don't wish to suggest that you ever ignore the rules and regulations under which you work when they are clearly highly relevant, but you strike me as a man with a practical attitude, one who would appreciate the futility of observing what is obviously futile.'

'I never leave my post without writing it down.'

'Do you realize how important your evidence is concerning the time at which my client left Hallam House?'

'Can't say.'

'If you insist you did not leave your post, even for a minute, just after seven o'clock, you are calling Mr Penfold a liar.'

'If he says he didn't see me, then he is.'

'By lying, you make it very much more difficult for him to prove that he is telling the truth from beginning to end.'

'I tell things like they was.'

Hindhead sat down.

Christine Ryan did not bother to re-examine.

Penfold garaged the car and walked towards the garden gate. After the adjournment, Hindhead had continued to express optimism, but it didn't take a mind-reader to judge the falsity of the words. Now it was his turn to simulate optimism when Lucy asked him how the day had gone and silently begged him to say it had gone well.

Sixteen

Christine Ryan began her cross-examination of Penfold late in the afternoon. 'I doubt I should be contradicted if I claimed your story of events to be one of the most unusual ever told in this courtroom.'

'It is not a story; it is what happened.' Penfold tried to speak calmly, but his voice betrayed the tension he was suffering.

'You claim you left Hallam House just after seven in the evening. Yet the security guard on duty failed to see you. Driving home, you were stopped by two cars and men in ski-masks blindfolded, bound and gagged you, and drove off with you wedged in the back of your Jaguar. You can offer not a shred of evidence to corroborate these extraordinary events. There can be no doubt – no doubt at all – that it was your car which struck and severely injured Mrs Lynch, yet you say you were not driving it at that time. No doubt you will claim it was pure coincidence that this accident took place on what was your normal route home from the office. Following the accident, you tell us your car was driven to a twenty-four-hour supermarket, where a litre bottle of whisky was purchased, your captors not having had the thoughtfulness to ask if you liked whisky. The car stopped in a lay-by and there you were forced to drink the contents of the bottle. What could be the motive for so bizarre an act except to render you unconscious or, at the very least, incapable? Then why drive you back to your house and abandon both car and you? You have forgotten the basic tenet that for a lie to be believed, it must enjoy at least the shadow of reality.'

131

'It's the truth,' he said for the second time, very conscious that now his voice was shadowed with hopelessness.

She picked up a sheet of paper, glanced at it and replaced it on the small stand in front of her. 'Do you drink alcohol, Mr Penfold?'

'If you're . . .' He abruptly stopped. Don't try to be smart, don't argue, don't say something in the heat of the moment that gives the prosecution ammunition; just answer the question as succinctly as possible. 'Yes.'

'Regularly?'

'It depends what you mean by that.'

'On the average day, would you drink some alcohol?'

'Not when I'm working; only after I've returned home.'

'You never visit a public house before lunch?'

'No. My work demands total concentration.'

'You would, perhaps, describe yourself as dedicated to your job?' She waited for him to answer; when he did not, she continued. 'Do you sometimes visit a public house after finishing work and before returning home?'

Hindhead rose. 'My Lord, the present line of questioning can only be intended to arouse prejudice.'

'Miss Ryan?' said the judge.

'My Lord, the accused is charged with driving and causing injury when under the influence of alcohol. Since it is generally recognized that alcohol will less quickly affect judgement if the drinker is a regular partaker of it, one would have thought my learned friend would welcome the suggestion that his client would not quickly be rendered incapable.'

'Since,' Hindhead said, 'my client was not driving his car either before, at or after the time of the accident, there can be no reason to try to determine just how quickly alcohol might affect him.'

'The allegation is that he was at the wheel when Mrs Lynch was injured. In the circumstances, the court is entitled to judge to what extent alcohol would be likely to affect his judgement.'

'He did not visit a public house after finishing work on the Friday.'

'The prosecution may raise the matter in general terms,' said the judge, annoyed that he should have to give the woman the benefit of doubt.

She addressed Penfold once more: 'Have you ever visited a public house after leaving Hallam House at the end of a working day?'

'I can't recall any specific time, but it is probable. In such circumstances, I would have restricted myself to one drink.'

'You would like to say you control your drinking carefully?'

'When I have to drive anywhere, yes.'

'Once at home, you allow yourself to be a little more indulgent?'

'I may have a drink before a meal, and wine with it.'

'And perhaps a liqueur afterwards?'

'Occasionally.'

'Have you always observed such admirable temperance?'

Hindhead stood. 'My Lord, there can really be no justification for my learned friend to continue this line of questioning.'

'I will allow this question, but unless counsel can give good reason for pursuing the subject, I will hold further questions to be inadmissible.'

Hindhead, accepting that to argue further might well do more harm than good, reluctantly sat.

'I will repeat the question,' she said: 'have you recently – say in the past three years – always drunk only temperately?'

Penfold suffered the panic of indecision. If she knew about the day at the Groves's, his affirmative could be proved a lie; if he admitted there had been the lunch when his drinking had resulted in his becoming obnoxiously drunk . . .

'You find it difficult to answer?'

'When I was younger, I sometimes drank more.'

'What do you mean by "younger"?'

Hindhead rose. 'My Lord . . .'

'Quite so,' said the judge. 'Miss Ryan, you will not pursue this line of questioning any further.'

'Very well, My Lord.' She was satisfied that in the minds of the jury had been planted the probability that Penfold's drinking had not always been so constrained as he now tried to make out.

'You say you left the office on Friday night almost immediately after you heard the church clock strike seven?' Christine Ryan said.

'Yes,' Penfold answered.

'You went down to the entrance hall, where you say you noticed Mr Cameron was not on duty at the control desk.'

'Yes.'

'You had reason to make certain whether or not he was there?'

'I always say goodnight to him.'

'Did you know that the security guard is required not to leave the control desk between the six and nine o'clock rounds except for very good reason?'

'Yes.'

'Then surely it would have crossed your mind that some good reason had called him away and that this might be serious?'

'No. I presumed he was making himself some tea.'

'Even though you knew that he was forbidden to do this at that time?'

'I knew he'd done just that more than once in the past.'

'You are accusing him of breaking the rules, even though your counsel praised him for his obvious attention to duty?'

'Making tea was a very minor breach of a stupid rule. If there'd been any kind of an alarm, he would have been back at the control desk within seconds.'

'You do not believe in observing rules and regulations?'

'I can sympathize with their non-observance when they are ridiculous.'

'And you think you have the right to judge that? . . . As Mr Cameron has told us, there was no alarm, no absence, no breach of rules. He has testified he was at the control desk from after his six o'clock round until nine and his log book bears him out.'

'Knowing he wasn't supposed to leave the desk, he wouldn't have made an entry of a brief absence.'

'You are, are you not, accusing Mr Cameron of having lied under oath – an act of perjury?'

'He is making the same accusation against me.'

'But he has less motive than you, doesn't he, to make such accusation?'

'Does he?'

'If you did leave Hallam House very soon after seven, as you claim, there was not the time, even for a hardened drinker, to become totally inebriated and in Oak Cross by seven thirty-five.'

'I think this is a good moment to adjourn,' the judge said.

Christine Ryan was a woman of spirit, yet managed to remain silent. The accused was becoming angry and flustered, and had she been allowed to continue her cross-examination, she might have provoked him into admitting the truth.

As the taxi turned into the drive of Alten Cobb, the outside light was switched on; by the time Penfold had paid the driver, Lucy was at the garden gate. 'Well?' she said breathlessly.

'The court adjourned while that woman was still cross-examining me,' he answered as he opened the gate and passed through.

'It's still not over?'

'Not yet.'

'Oh, God! I'd so hoped . . . How's it been, darling?'

For the first time, he could express his feelings. 'I couldn't help letting her annoy me. Looking and acting like Boudicca on the charge, calling me a liar over and over again, sneering, digging up the dirt . . .'

'What dirt?'

'My drinking history.'

'What's that to do with what happened?'

'Helps her persuade the jury I was drinking heavily of my own free will and my version of what happened is an attempt to hide the truth.'

'Why didn't Hindhead stop her?'

'He tried, but the judge let her go on and on. Obviously has a soft spot for her,' he added bitterly.

Seventeen

C hristine Ryan leaned forward and spoke to her instructing solicitor at some length.

'Are you intending to continue with your cross-examination?' the judge asked, pleased to have the opportunity to admonish her in judicial terms.

'With Your Lordship's permission,' she answered, as she straightened up. She faced Penfold once more, the lines of her face slightly more marked – there was always strain in a long cross-examination. 'You say that after the phone call made on a mobile, the men were ordered to drive to a nearby all-night supermarket and there to buy a litre bottle of whisky?'

'Yes,' Penfold answered. She was speaking pleasantly and in no way accusingly, yet he was bitterly certain that her manner would be seen – and was meant to be seen – by the jury as portraying unbiased patience in the face of lying stupidity.

'To fit inside the time scale, as has been shown, this supermarket has to be one of the two twenty-four-hour ones on the outskirts of Pettersgrove. You cannot say which it was?'

'Being blindfolded and shoved down into the well of the car, no.'

'If one wishes to drive from Hallam House to Fieldhurst, does the direct and quickest route pass through Oak Cross?'

'Yes.'

'Is it the route you normally take?'

'Yes. And he returned to it after making a wrong turn earlier on.'

'To whom are you referring?'

'The man who was driving my car. He was told to return to where he'd made a mistake and start again, but decided he could find his way back on to the right route cross-country without doing that.'

'I don't remember your mentioning this in your examination-in-chief.'

'I've only just remembered it.'

'How fortunate memory should return just in time to explain why your car passed through Oak Cross when you were in it, but not driving it. After all, Oak Cross is an obscure place and it would be surprising if kidnappers wanting to make a quick getaway had not preferred to make use of the readily accessible A roads.'

He spoke wildly. 'From the moment they grabbed me, I've been in Kafka land and unable to think straight. So however much you sneer at me—'

'I'm sorry if you mistakenly think I am in any way sneering at you. My sole objective is to establish the truth in a manner the court can understand. And to do that it is necessary for them to appreciate how a man could forget something one would expect to be emblazoned on his mind—'

Hindhead rose and interrupted her. 'I was not aware, My Lord, that we had reached the stage of delivering our closing speeches.'

'Nor was I,' agreed the judge, delighted to criticize without disclosing a bias that might justify an appeal.

'My Lord,' she said, 'what I was attempting to do was to present matters in a manner which could be understood by all.'

'Then perhaps you might do so more succinctly.'

She faced the witness box once more. 'You have, perhaps fortuitously, remembered that the men whom you claim kidnapped you lost their way and as a result of this, drove along the route you would normally and logically have taken from Hallam House to your home.'

The interruption had enabled him to regain a measure of self-control. 'Yes,' he answered shortly.

'And after Mrs Lynch was knocked to the ground, the car was driven to a supermarket, where a bottle of whisky was bought, which you were made to drink?'

'Yes.'

'Did you understand why you were being subjected to such extraordinary treatment?'

'No.'

'Not one of the men said anything that enabled you to begin to surmise their motive?'

'No.'

'And since that time, when you have been asked to suggest what that motive might have been, what has been your answer?'

'That it must somehow have been connected with my work.'

'If that were so, why should they have left you at your house before they had made even the slightest use of your computer expertise?'

'After the accident, they knew the police would be trying to identify the car and, if successful, would realize some form of theft was intended in which my skills would play the major part. Then they would not only take steps to prevent that from happening, but would be aware that a similar attempt might be made in the future.'

'Do you have any proof to back up your assumptions?'

'No.'

'Then you would find it difficult to counter the possibility that your suggestions are merely an attempt to meet the questions which common sense must raise?'

'You asked me what the motive could be and I've told you what I think.'

'Perhaps you are to be congratulated on your mental ingenuity . . . When you recovered consciousness after returning home, you must have been very worried?'

'I'd no idea of what had happened until my wife told me what the police had said. I couldn't believe it.'

'Did you not say in your examination-in-chief that, during the journey and before you were forced to drink the whisky, you felt the car hit something and from the panicky comments of your fellow travellers, you understood someone had been hit?'

'Yes, but . . .'

'But?'

'It was all so crazy that the next morning I thought maybe my wife had misheard the police. I couldn't believe anyone would think I'd been driving my car; it was just too incredible.'

'I cannot think of a more apposite work than "incredible".'

'Everything I've said is the truth.'

'Byron wrote: ". . . for truth is always strange;/Stranger than fiction." Were he present, I suggest he would amend those lines: "Good fiction should be strange; stranger than the truth."'

Hindhead half-rose. 'I think, My Lord, Byron would at least make certain the words scanned.'

'I am glad to say that it is not part of our remit to judge the quality of the works of a deceased poet's amanuensis, so we will proceed.'

She wondered whether the male members of the Bar and bench would ever understand how absurd their snide, juvenile comments sounded. 'Mr Penfold, I suggest you left Hallam House well before seven, visited a bar or bars where you consumed a considerable amount of alcohol and set out to drive home on the route you normally took. In Oak Cross you struck and seriously injured Mrs Lynch. Frightened of the consequences of what had happened, ignoring the fact that failing to give help might have fatal consequences for the victim, you fled. In your drunken fear, seeking false courage, you stopped in the lay-by and there drank heavily from a bottle of whisky – despite your assertion and your wife's evidence that you dislike whisky – which you kept in the car. You arrived home in a state of drunkenness, but were able to explain to your wife what had happened. She, showing the loyalty many wives mistakenly offer their husbands, decided to help you by claiming, when the police arrived, that you were ill from natural causes and were not drunk. Later, when you had sufficiently recovered, your wife informed you the police had been to the house and a blood sample had been taken from you; you understood that this must prove beyond argument the very large amount of alcohol you had consumed. You desperately cast around for an explanation that would relieve you of guilt and decided to offer the implausible story we have been asked to believe . . . Is that not the truth?'

'I did not have a drink before the men stopped my car. I was blindfolded, gagged and shoved down into the well when Mrs Lynch was struck.'

'Imagination and truth make poor bedfellows.'

'Are we to be told whose works you are adapting this time, Miss Ryan?' the judge asked.

'Ill-favoured words, sir, but mine own.'

'Well?' Lucy asked anxiously.

He watched the taxi drive along the lane, its progress marked by headlights.

'Aren't you going to tell me?'

'I'm still being cross-examined. The case is adjourned until Monday.'

'Why is it going on and on?'

'Justice is normally pictured as blindfolded as she holds the scales; she ought to be given earplugs as well. They won't listen; they won't bloody listen. Just because their lives have always been smooth, they refuse to understand that something can suddenly turn the world upside down. I can't . . .' He belatedly realized his wild words must have made her fear the case was slowly, inexorably going against him and he tried, however futilely, to make her believe there was still hope. As they walked to the garden gate, he told her what Hindhead had said – words Hindhead had never spoken.

When they were seated in the priest's room, she said, 'Charles rang earlier.'

'Is something wrong?'

'It's become common knowledge you're in court and the other boys are jeering at him and saying . . .' She began to cry.

He crossed and sat on the arm of her chair, held her against himself.

'They're saying he'll soon be the son of a jailbird . . . How can they be so viciously nasty?'

He remembered his days at prep school. One boy had suffered a weak bladder and slept on a bag of absorbent material. Constantly jeered at, he'd once had his face rubbed on the bag. Penfold tried to tell himself he'd not been one of those tormentors, but he could not be certain.

On Monday, Penfold's cross-examination was completed and his re-examination began. At four fifty, the court was adjourned.

Christine Ryan left the robing room and, red bag in her left hand, walked down the corridor to the nearest exit. Her instructing solicitor joined her.

'Looks as if it's virtually over,' he said.

'I suppose so.'

'You've doubts?' He began to breathe more heavily because she walked quickly and he was overweight and had been out of condition for longer than he cared to remember.

'Not exactly. Yet I can't escape the possibility he's telling the truth, however ridiculous it sounds.'

'Do you think the defence may pull something out of the hat?'

'I doubt that.' She opened the door before he could reach it and went out into the dreary, dampening November evening. 'What's troubling me is probably only feminine intuition.'

'Better not offer that to Mr Justice Brown.'

They laughed and went their separate ways.

Hindhead called two character witnesses, one of whom was Lucy's father. Smartly dressed, with a clipped accent, he had served in the Guards; he was a leader who had always had genuine regard for those he led. In the witness box he gave it as his opinion that his son-in-law was incapable of acting as alleged; had he unfortunately injured someone, he would immediately have called an ambulance; had he been guilty, he would have admitted that fact, because he was a man of honour.

As he stepped down from the witness box, Hindhead admitted to himself that it had been a mistake to call him. For so many years the old values had been denigrated that most, perhaps all, of the jury would have seen the witness as a pompous duffer trying to save his own kind at the expense of an elderly woman.

Hindhead's closing speech came to an end – an inconclusive end, since it was difficult to make bricks without straw or clay. Christine Ryan's was longer, as she quietly, carefully, detailed every piece of evidence and how it fitted into the whole picture.

Mr Justice Brown's summing-up continued into the Wednesday – he was always careful to give due weight to any evidence in favour of the accused and he did like the sound of his own voice.

The jury retired to consider their verdict.

The foreman was asked whether the jury had reached a verdict? They had: Guilty.

Eighteen

From outside it looked like an ordinary van; inside were six small compartments, three on either side, divided by metal bars. As Penfold climbed into the very narrow way between the cages, aided by an unnecessary push in the back and a shout of 'Hurry it up, you're not at bleeding Ascot', he suffered the first icy humiliation of imprisonment. He went into the nearest cage to the left, was called a stupid bastard and ordered into the furthest one. The man on his right drooled and muttered over and over again words which appeared to be some sort of prayer.

He sat on the wooden board. He had been allowed to make one phone call before being led out to the van. He'd told Lucy he had been found guilty and sentenced to five years' imprisonment. Her cries of shocked disbelief had made him fear she would collapse. He'd tried to make a second call, to ask a friend to help her . . . Didn't he understand? One call meant one call, not a bleeding dozen. But his wife needed help . . . Too right, she did, married to a boofhead like him. Move . . .

The van started with a jerk that caused one of the other four prisoners to fall off the seat; the man next to him laughed. Another prisoner began to bang his head against the side of the van, shouting meaninglessly as he did so.

Someone – and his mind was so confused that he couldn't remember who – had told him that if he caused no trouble, he'd only have to do two-thirds of his sentence. Three and a third years – for a crime he hadn't committed. It couldn't happen in a democracy. It couldn't bloody well happen . . .

Hindhead had talked about an appeal, but with little enthusiasm – probably thinking that if he had had even a little intelligence, he'd have thought up a story that stood at least a small chance of being believed . . .

For just over twelve hundred days Lucy would have to face on her own a world that knew him as a convicted criminal. Tradition said she would learn who were their true friends. Would there prove to be any? *Schadenfreude* was a very descriptive German word; he knew of no English word that so concisely depicted the trait of gaining pleasure from denigrating and isolating someone who had once prospered, but did so no longer . . .

After a twenty-five-minute drive, they entered the court-yard of HM Prison, Whiteleigh. Seldom had anywhere been less appropriately named. Built a hundred and fifty years before, its high outside walls and ugly brick buildings were grimed with dirt. He was to learn there was far more dirt inside.

A warder, who seemed capable only of shouting, ordered them to undress, put their clothes in the bags provided, shower, put on prison clothes, queue to be medically examined, queue to speak to the psychiatrist, queue to speak to the governor or assistant governor – remembering to address those gentlemen as 'sir' or there would be sodding trouble. After that, they were to go to their cells, where they'd be banged up for the night. Grub? They wanted to know when they'd be having some grub? Did they think this was the sodding Ritz? They should have been fed before they left the courthouse and since it was now too late, they were going to stay hungry until the morning.

The shower water was lukewarm. The prison clothes looked, and in some cases smelled, as if they had not been cleaned since last worn. The physical examination was embarrassing and degrading. The psychiatrist was fussy, almost bald, and annoyed because he had had to stay at the prison because of their late arrival. Did Penfold understand he had been found guilty of a crime . . . Yes, yes, every prisoner was innocent . . . and he had been sent to prison not solely as a punishment, but also to learn and understand the need for repentance and, through understanding, become a better person? Did his family know he was in prison? There might be times when he would be tempted to resist the rules, but he should understand that these were laid down for the good of all prisoners.

The assistant governor skimmed through the report in front of him, looked up. It was always a shame to meet a man who had abused his position of privilege . . . Yes, yes, every prisoner was innocent . . . There would be no privilege in prison. Obey the rules and he would find life hard but fair; disobey them and he must expect serious trouble. Next prisoner.

Escorted by a warder, a sullen-looking man who said nothing beyond roughly directing him along passages and through doorways that had to be unlocked, to a square – a primitive atrium covered with heavy netting at each floor to prevent suicides – up steel stairs, past cells whose doors were open, to D56.

Rabbits were kept in more spacious captivity, he thought as he entered, not then realizing he was fortunate to be in one of the small cells on each floor, since there were only two bunks. Sitting on the chair, leafing through a magazine of comics, was a small man whose thin, greasy hair topped a mean, ill-proportioned face which had an air of slyness; when he opened his mouth, it was to expose missing or blackened teeth.

'Yours, Ellis,' said the warder, as if delivering a parcel. He left, treading heavily to invest himself with additional authority.

'What's the handle, mate? Mine's Tom,' Ellis said, in a high-pitched, whining voice.

Penfold did not immediately reply. To have to share a cell with this flotsam of humanity . . .

'What's your grief? Ain't dumb, is you?'

'Just disorientated.'

Ellis looked at him with astonishment.

'Which is my bunk?'

Ellis pointed at the lower one.

Penfold dropped the small plastic bag in which were the toothbrush, toothpaste, flannel, soap and very flexible comb he had been issued, on the bunk. He sat, hunched up to avoid hitting his head. Black despair gripped him.

'What's your special, then?'

'How d'you mean?' he asked listlessly.

'What gets a bloke like you banged up?'

'Banged up?'

'Don't you know your arse from your elbow? If you wasn't here, I'd say you'd been done for a perv. I'm asking why you's inside?'

'I've been convicted of drunken driving, knocking a woman down and severely injuring her.'

'What was you boozed on? Fizz?' He sounded envious.

'I wasn't driving the car.'

'Must of been or you wouldn't be inside, would you?'

'No one would believe the truth.'

'Them sods never do.' He hawked. 'Didn't believe me when they nicked me the last time. Which they wouldn't of done if the bastard hadn't grassed me . . . You ain't said your name.'

'Gavin.'

'Not what the screws call you, what I calls you.'

'Gavin is my Christian name.'

'Yeah? Sounds kind of glitzy. Could say it goes along with the likes of you, I suppose. How much bird you got?'

'Bird?'

'How long are you inside?'

'Five years.'

'Same as me. Makes us mates, don't it?'

Could there be anyone he would less have welcomed as a mate?

'I shouldn't have got that much stretch. Only the bastard wig said as I was a danger to the public. Me a danger, when all I did was teach the sod? . . . You done a lot of schooling?'

'Enough.'

'So you read easy?'

'Yes.'

'I don't.'

There was a brief silence.

'D'you want to help a mate?' Ellis asked.

'If I can,' Penfold lied.

'Read me something, 'cause I ain't so good at it.'

'What would you like me to read?'

Ellis stood, crossed to the bunks and reached to the upper one. It had to be imagination, but Penfold seemed to smell rat. Ellis backed away and held out a letter in his right hand.

'You want me to read that?'

'From me gash. Writes regular and it ain't everyone what does. Like Lofty. Ain't heard from his in weeks and he says if she's kneeling for someone else, he'll have the bastard's nuts on a toasting fork when he gets out.'

Reluctantly – never read anyone else's letters had been one of his childhood injunctions – Penfold took the envelope and brought out two sheets of paper whose four sides were covered in a handwritten scrawl.

Ellis sat once more. 'There ain't another like Hazel.'

Penfold began to read aloud. After two sentences he stopped.

'What's up? Ain't in trouble, is she?'

'What she's writing is . . . rather personal.'

'Didn't I say there ain't another? I go home and she's over me before I gets the front door shut.'

'I don't think she'd welcome anyone but you knowing what she's written, because it's becoming very . . . specific.'

'How d'you mean?'

Absurdly, Penfold was embarrassed. 'She describes . . .
well, very intimate details of what she . . .'

'Does she tell what she wants to do with me?'

'It seems possible.'

'Go on, then.'

'Are you certain you want me to know what she's written?'

'You're me mate, ain't you? If you don't read, I won't
know, and she'll be real sad if I wasn't thinking of her doing
all the things she says.'

As Penfold read on, his amazement increased; it seemed
he and Lucy had led very sheltered lives.

All cell lights had been turned out; through the barred
inspection square in the door, sufficient light entered to
enable most of the interior details to be made out.

This time last night, Penfold thought . . . He silently swore.
If he were to survive the present, he could not dare live in
the past. But what Hazel had written in the letter goaded
memories. Before turning off the bedside lights, he and Lucy
always kissed goodnight. Quite often their sleepiness slid
away and they once more discovered the renewal of love
that sex provided . . .

'Have you got another handle?'

He stared up at the shadowy underneath of the upper bunk.
Memory could stretch more fiercely than the rack, crush more
painfully than *peine forte et dure*.

'You ain't asleep, is you, Gavin?'

'If I had been, I wouldn't be now.'

'How's that?'

'No, I'm not asleep.'

'Then has you another handle?'

'Are you asking me if I have a second Christian name?'

'Ain't that what I just said?'

'My second name is John.'

'You'd best use that inside.'

'Why?'

'Because there's some what will think, if you're Gavin, you're a battyman.'

'And who or what is a battyman?'

'Gawd! It's like talking to a kid what's still on his mum's tits. A birdie, a bufu, a jam duff, a poofta.'

How sad his father would have been to learn the inference some might draw from the family christian name. According to his father, Gavin was the Scottish form of Gawain, the Arthurian knight – the most noble of provenances.

'If you ain't careful, Johnny, you're going to have it rough.'

He'd already come to that conclusion.

Clemens hurried into the CID general room, a sheet of paper in his right hand. 'Where's Tom?'

'Had to have a word with uniform, Sarge,' Young answered.

'Why?'

'Can't rightly say.'

'Because the truth is, he hasn't reported in yet?'

'He was dead on time.'

'And Elvis was with him, talking about his hound dogs . . . When he does honour us with his presence, tell him I want a word. And Ernie, you take off to twenty-four, Carnforth Lane – that's to the south – and get a witness statement from Peter Cornley. Seems he saw a vehicle accident in Baslingdon and the locals need his evidence.' Clemens began to walk towards the doorway, stopped and turned back. 'Any of you know if there's been a verdict in the Penfold case yet?'

'Yesterday evening,' Myers answered. 'Jury wasn't out long enough to confuse themselves. Judge handed out a fiver. Should have been a tenner.' He turned to Kendrick. 'Not soft enough still to think he wasn't driving?'

'It's just . . .' Kendrick began.

'Just that you knuckle your forehead and think he can do as

150

he wants. Wouldn't surprise me if you even reckon he ought to have first dip of the village maidens.'

'I still don't understand . . .' Kendrick began.

'Because if you see a bloke hot-wiring a car, you go up and ask him if he's lost his key.'

'I'd like to know why he said what he did.'

'And for that much, so would I,' Clemens said. 'Seems real odd, a man like him offering a story a five-year-old would laugh at. But I don't suppose we'll ever know the answer.' He left the room.

'The one essential qualification for a detective sergeant,' Myers said, 'is to be as thick as two oak planks.'

'So you're applying for promotion?' Young spoke more thoughtfully. 'I wonder how Penfold is coping when he's suffering just about as big a change in circumstances as one can. If he's really innocent, it'll be double hell for him.'

'He's just learning what life's like for the rest of us,' Myers said ill-temperedly.

Nineteen

The inmates formed a long, untidy, restless queue that stretched from the cafeteria out into the main hall; warders watched, ready to dampen down any minor incident before it risked becoming a major one that could expose the fragility of their authority. In the queue, there were eddies of movement as men talked, argued and verbally challenged each other. One such eddy caught Penfold off-balance and he cannoned into a younger man whose most noticeable feature was a four-inch scar across his right cheek.

'I'm sorry,' Penfold said, as he regained his balance.

He was cursed for his clumsiness with violent crudeness.

His response was immediate, born of an instinctive resentment at having his apology rejected. 'Look, I really couldn't help what happened . . .'

The man's fist landed in his side and although it had travelled only a few inches, the pain doubled him up.

'Stand up,' Ellis said urgently. 'The screws are watching.' Using what strength he had, he helped Penfold upright.

One of the warders, an elderly man who possessed the skill of being able to treat prisoners with a degree of friendliness without being thought weak, came across.

'Something the matter?' he asked as the queue partially disintegrated and inmates crowded around them.

About to explain he'd been viciously assaulted, Penfold was forestalled by Ellis. 'No problem, Mr Yelton. Johnny gets these pains sometimes.'

Yelton asked Penfold, 'What sort of pains?'

152

'It comes and goes,' Ellis answered.

'So would you like to go and leave the man to answer for himself?' He turned back. 'What's your name?'

'Penfold.'

'How long have you been suffering these pains?'

'Often,' said Ellis.

'Did you hear me?'

'Yes, Mr Yelton.'

'But it's asking too much for you to keep quiet? . . . Best see the doctor, Penfold, and make certain there's nothing serious.'

'What happened was—'

'Do like he says, Johnny,' Ellis cut in urgently. 'See the croaker and tell him how the pain comes and goes.'

'Especially when you get in the way of someone?' Yelton turned and made his way back to where he had previously stood.

'You've a right one there, Ratty,' a nearby inmate observed. 'He's fresh.'

'If he ain't bleeding careful, he'll soon be stale and rotting.'

Later, in their cell, Ellis said, 'Jeeze, Johnny, you near had me dunking in me shoes. You was going to tell the screw what happened, wasn't you?'

'Of course I was.'

Ellis looked at Penfold with sad disbelief. 'Don't they teach you nothing where you comes from?'

'If someone assaults me, I complain to authority.'

'It ain't bleeding possible!'

'Aren't the warders there to maintain order?'

'Don't you have no whisper of what would of happened if you'd narked? Ain't no one never told you what happens to narks?'

'No.'

'If they're lucky, they just gets duffed, their phone cards nicked, their kit bust; if they ain't, they's chivved so heavy, it's like doing a jig-saw to put the bits together again; or maybe they're glass-eyed. Ain't never seen someone what's been stretched?'

'If I couldn't tell the warder what happened, what was I supposed to do? Smile? Or hit back?'

'When it was Larry the Scar what belted you?'

'That makes a difference?'

'He's a hatchet man what runs a mob outside. Two years back, there was some what thought of taking over his territory; three disappeared and the coppers still ain't found them . . . Hit him and you'd be in hospital wondering if there was any part of you still working.'

'And three or four dozen people would have been watching and not one of them would have seen what happened?'

'You're learning, Johnny, you're learning, but it ain't fast enough.'

Bells sounded: main lights would be switched off in fifteen minutes.

Later, after they were on their bunks and in the dim night light, Ellis said, 'You want to walk out at the other end, don't you?'

'Do I wish to survive my imprisonment? Yes.'

'Then stop speaking glitzy. Sounds like you think yourself better than the likes of us.'

'Which couldn't be further from the truth.'

'There you are! Like the sodding aristo what investigates the nick and walks around with the governor and asks if we've complaints. So dumb, he don't know that if we said we'd got plenty, the screws'd make certain we was in solitary before his car was out of sight. You've got to talk more natural.'

'I'll do my best.'

'Be one of us and you'll find mates, especially as I been telling how you'll read letters or write appeals to the parole board or be a mouthpiece for them what wants.'

Penfold guiltily remembered how he had initially viewed Ellis with dislike and contempt.

*   *   *

154

He was placed on washroom-cleaning duty. He was given a manual that detailed his duties and how they were to be carried out; the prisoner whose washroom was, on governor's rounds, judged the cleanest would receive a bonus in pay.

'You're dead lucky to get that soft a number,' Ellis told him.

One's values could experience astonishing change, Penfold thought.

'You need to watch, though.'

'Watch what?'

'That you keep your eyes shut sodding tight.'

About to point out that it would be difficult to watch with his eyes shut, he remembered such comments were not appreciated inside. 'What's the problem?'

'It's where the deals is done.'

'What deals?'

'Booze and gold dust, charlie, hop, kif – what's your choice?'

'Drugs?'

'They ain't peppermint bars.'

'There's drug-taking in prison?'

'One day, Johnny, you'll maybe say something what doesn't give me a hernia laughing.'

After a week of washroom duty, Penfold knew who sold drugs and who used them (cigarettes were one currency and phone cards another; credit was available for those who felt sufficiently confident they would never suffer the consequences of welshing on their debts); who sold alcohol and who risked intestinal destruction by drinking what they bought. Buyer and seller would, separately, drift into the washroom. Most would nod a brief greeting to Penfold before conducting their business as quickly as possible. Those with outside backing – heavies ready to support them – conscious of their social standing, would usually nod again when they left; those with no real backing would often offer him a drink, a cigarette, perhaps even a small fix, as a sweetener that would ensure his silence not only in respect of authority, but also with competitors; his polite refusals of all offers confused and alarmed until they accepted that these presaged no ulterior motive.

Ellis's warning became sharply relevant on a Friday morning. The head warder and four companions rushed into the washroom, grabbed hold of the two prisoners trading and one buying who were present, searched them and, finding alcohol and heroin, led them away to appear before the governor on charges.

At lunch, seated at one of the bare, stained wooden tables, Ellis leaned forward and, speaking quietly yet audibly despite the general hubbub that was increased by an echo – a knack quickly learned – said to Penfold, 'Is that gospel? The screws busted your turf?'

'Five of them came in and took the three who were marketing.'

'Who were they?'

'Barney, Alec and Slim.'

'Shit!'

'There's a panic?'

Ellis lowered his head and shovelled into his mouth the remaining food on the plastic, sectioned plate.

Later, when they were in the main recreational area, seated near the table tennis, Ellis said: 'Johnny, you didn't grass 'em, did you? It weren't you what brought the screws into the khazi?'

'Of course not.'

'You never said nothing to any screw?'

'Not half a whisper.'

'There's likely be some . . .'

An argument between the table tennis players over the score became heated; warders hurried across and separated the four men.

'Best move,' Ellis said.

Penfold followed him towards the area where men played

disorganized basketball or walked in strange geometric patterns as if their minds had blanked. When they reached the far wall, Ellis said, 'You got to watch real hard.'

'For what?'

'You still don't understand?'

'Tell me.'

'Them three what got nicked and lost gear will be up before the governor and they'll be done on remission and maybe spend time in Siberia. Barney thinks himself real sharp so won't see it was his own sodding stupid fault for not leaving eyes outside to bell an alarm if screws looked interested. He'll say they was grassed by you.'

'Why the hell would I do that?'

'To earn with the governor. So like I said, watch solid. Don't go near the khazi . . .'

'Aren't you forgetting, that's my job?'

'See the croaker and tell him your back's bad so as you can't do no more mopping and polishing.'

'But—'

'Johnny, don't you want to stay healthy?'

'If any of them is stupid enough to accuse me of grassing, I'll explain I didn't and it was just bad luck the screws mounted the raid when they did.'

'I don't reckon even a head-shrinker could do you no good.'

He was carefully polishing the brass taps – to his astonishment, he had become proud of the condition of the washroom – when two men entered. He recognized Alec, but not the other. Each held a favourite prison weapon – Alec, a lavatory brush with the bristles replaced with razor blades; his companion, a plastic table knife with the end shaped and shaved to make it a stabbing dagger that in skilled hands could be as dangerous as if made of metal.

A man left one of the cubicles, immediately sized up the situation and ran out of the washroom. Alec, small, wiry, his volcanic temper responsible for his fifteen-year sentence, approached Penfold with crabwise steps. 'You won't be grassing no more,' he said violently, spittle spraying out as he spoke.

'I haven't grassed . . .'

He was interrupted by a flood of obscenity.

'I swear I've not spoken to any screw . . .' he began.

'You ain't going to tell no screw nothing more.' Alec sliced the air with the brush.

All but numbed with fear, he decided to shout for help, no matter what the consequences of alerting the warders . . .

The swing doors were thrown back as two men entered – men who looked as if they'd spent much of their lives in body-building training. Many still spoke of the arm-wrestling competition in which they'd met in the final: a draw had been declared after twenty minutes. Norman, the taller of the two by a quarter of an inch, built on hickory lines, jerked his head in the direction of the doorway. 'Get.'

'What's it to you?' Alec demanded.

He didn't answer.

'It's not your grief.'

He spat his contempt.

'He grassed.'

'Get or I'll shove your piece up your butt.'

For a few seconds Alec did nothing; then he crossed to the door, closely followed by his companion.

As the doors swung shut behind them, Penfold became aware of the sweat that dampened his shirt. With the stupidity that could follow fear, he thought it had taken fellow inmates to rescue him because warders, like policemen, were never on hand when one needed them.

'I said, don't go to the khazi.' Ellis spoke with shrill annoyance.

'I didn't realize . . . I didn't think that anything like this could happen in prison.'

'When they put the likes of you inside, they ought to learn you first.'

'Thank God those two came in when they did or I'd have been badly injured.'

'You think God sent 'em? I've seen kids with more brains.'

'It was you?'

'Course it bleeding well was. Alec always talks big and was telling how he'd mark you something terrible, so I kept me eyes open, and when he and Ted moved to the khazi what you was in, I told Norm and Phil to break things up.'

'I must thank them.'

'With a century for each.'

'I need to pay them?'

'You reckon they did it 'cause they likes you?'

'I suppose not,' Penfold answered slowly. 'But how can I pay them when I'm inside?'

'You ain't skint outside, so you gets a century to each of 'em where they says they wants it. And you does it quick or they'll be apeshit with the both of us. And I've said there's another ten centuries each if you don't have no trouble all the time you're here. With them doing the minding, there ain't going to be no one starts trouble, however crazy you are.'

It seemed that while he'd never needed bodyguards when out of prison, he did now he was inside one.

The visiting hall was as bleak as the thoughts of those in it. Wooden tables, with plastic barriers a foot high across the centre, were set in rows; the three large windows were protected with metal grilles; the walls, painted in two shades of institutional brown, were bare; warders stood at different points or moved around as they kept sharp watch on all that happened; one or two women were always quietly weeping . . .

'No physical contact,' said the warder at the inner door, a rule that had not been enforced until a woman had been caught using her tongue to pass a small pack of heroin to her man as she kissed him.

As Penfold entered, his eyes suddenly misted and he was unable to distinguish features until he had blinked several times . . . Lucy sat halfway along the third row of tables. As he approached, he felt as if he had swallowed ice.

She tried to smile, but her lips were trembling. He sat and for several seconds no words were spoken; then his were banal: 'How are things?'

'Not so bad . . . And you?'

'As they say, when you've been to an English boarding school, prison is a doddle.'

She visually searched his face. 'You look . . .'

'Fit from regular exercise and not sitting in front of a VDU all day long.'

'George told me your appeal will take some time to be heard. I asked him to try to hurry it up.'

'Asking the law to hurry is like asking Michelin Man to run.'

'He says Mr Hindhead is quite optimistic.'

Waite could be blunt and he had probably told her she should not pin too much faith on a rapid or successful appeal. 'How's Charles?'

'I had a long talk with Burrows over the phone. It seems initially there were some boys who jeered at Charles – you knew that, didn't you? – but then he told everyone you were really in jail for stealing a fortune from the bank, but they won't admit that because it would make them look so stupid. When you come out, you'll be so rich you'll drive a Ferrari and we'll live in Tuscany in such style the Prime Minister will ask to be invited. Now the boys are envying Charles.'

'Thereby defeating any attempt to teach them the moral value of honesty.'

'Burrows remarked that boys as well as God move in a mysterious way.'

'I've always thought his greatest asset is that he can keep

a sense of humour even in the face of a hundred and fifty barbarians . . . There's something important I'd like you to do as soon as you can – that is, to send a hundred pounds in cash to two addresses which I'll give you, and to stand by to send more money later on. Have you got paper and pencil handy?'

'I had to leave my handbag outside. It made me so angry. They're trying to humiliate us.'

'It's much more likely a case of precaution. Allow handbags in here and half the inmates would be high by tonight.'

'What do you mean?'

'Drugs would have been passed to them.'

'Surely no one would think of doing such a thing?'

It was ironic how her innocence now seemed so naive to him. 'I'll give you the addresses when I write – I'm allowed to send you a letter tomorrow.'

'Oh God! They even ration letters?'

'Everything they can control, they do. If there was a machine to control thinking, they'd buy thousands.' He realized he was in danger of betraying some of his misery. 'But I guess they'd have to wait because the politicians would demand first call.'

'Who's the money for?'

'Minding.'

'What's that mean? Gavin, you're talking in a way that's difficult to understand.'

'Sorry, darling. But when you find yourself in Rome, it's a distinct advantage to talk as the Romans do.'

'Then . . . then things aren't . . .'

'Nearly as bad as they could be, thanks to my cellmate. He's guided me through the initiation ceremonies. How are your parents responding to events?'

'They've been wonderfully supportive.'

'As I expected they would.'

'Other people have been . . . different.'

'Also as expected.'

'Beatrice . . .' She stopped.

161

'In that sweet, soft, syrupy voice, and in the most refined way possible, she's bitchily made it clear you're off her welcome list?'

'I was quite rude to her.'

'Not before time. I'll guarantee Alice has behaved very differently.'

'She took me out to lunch at the new fish restaurant because she said I looked like I was dissolving.'

They chatted, much as they would have done at home, and for a while this allowed them to ignore their surroundings.

A bell rang loudly and discordantly. Visitors left. Penfold was certain that after her last wave, when she had turned away, her tears had begun. He experienced the raging anger of total helplessness.

Some months later, Penfold was informed by the assistant governor that he was to be transferred to West Antrem, an open prison.

'Lucky bastard,' Ellis said. 'More like a holiday camp than doing bird. Day release and all.'

'Maybe they'll move you soon.'

'When I got mine for duffing up that sod with a bottle? Once you're marked violent, there ain't no easy times.'

Ellis had never detailed the nature of, or the reason for, his conviction. 'What made you beat up someone?' Penfold asked curiously.

Ellis, as far as his shifty character allowed, was embarrassed. He twice looked quickly at Penfold and then away before he said, 'You wouldn't broadcast, would you?'

'No snitching.'

'It was like this, see . . .' He became silent, looked quickly at Penfold once more. 'Hazel kind of liked him. Used to laugh a lot with him and kept asking me why I was so gloomy. Ain't easy to laugh when you sees your woman laughing with another bloke. Then I comes home sudden and they're together and her knickers is on the floor. She swore the dog

had brought 'em down from upstairs. Ted just laughed. Big
bloke – not as big as Norm, of course, but a sight bigger'n
me. Said how much he'd enjoyed himself before he cleared
off. Hazel swore he was just talking big because he'd tried
it on and she'd refused. I believed her. She wasn't no tart.
You understand that, don't you, Johnny?'

'Of course I do.'

'Then I heard Ted was boasting how she was the hottest
lay he'd ever had and how he couldn't wait for more. I
wasn't having him blacking Hazel. He used to pub at the
Golden Goose, so I waited for him to come out and used
a bottle. He still wasn't out of hospital when they shoved
me inside.' He paused, then said urgently, 'You won't tell
about Hazel?'

'I've already promised. But why the panic? It's only what
anyone else would have done.'

'You still ain't learned! I've been telling that him and me
fell out over what we'd nicked and he tried to con me of my
share, so I did him good and proper; that's earned me noise.
If they was to learn it was because of him and Hazel . . .
They'd laugh and I'd lose all me noise.'

Penfold collected up the few things he would be taking
with him. 'I'm sorry you're not coming with me, Ratty.'

'You'll be square, Johnny. I taught you good.'

'You did indeed.'

'You and me will be out near the same time . . .'

'Yes?'

'It was me thinking bleeding daft.'

'What were you going to say?'

'If you's ever in Tellsbury, we could have a jar or two
together.'

'We'll tear the town apart.'

They were both certain they would never meet again.

Twenty

Thanks to release days during the time Penfold was in the open prison, his final freedom was not the potentially unnerving experience it might have been; nevertheless, as Lucy drove the Astra away from the gates that marked the prison boundary, he seemed to be entering a different world.

'I just can't believe you won't have to go back.' Lucy's voice was choky.

'Then stop the car.'

She braked to a halt at the side of the road. He kissed her. The driver of a passing van hooted his approval.

'I've been waiting a lifetime for that.' Her voice had steadied.

'Twelve hundred and seventeen days.'

'Have you remembered the leap year and which months have less than thirty-one days?'

'Probably not.'

She released the handbrake, engaged first, waited for a car to pass and drew back on to the road. 'I did wonder whether you'd like a celebratory lunch at Frascatti's, but decided you'd prefer home. I hope I was right?'

'A hundred per cent – a hundred and one per cent if the menu is smoked salmon, leg of lamb, and lemon meringue pie.'

'How did I guess?'

'Fourteen years of married hard labour.'

'Eleven of heaven, three and a third of hell.'

He stared out at the occasional farm house, hedges and trees beginning to leaf, and fields green with new grass or crops, and thought that one had to visit hell in order fully to appreciate heaven.

In the priest's room he switched off the cordless phone and put it down on the small pie-crust table at the side of the chair. 'Charles sounded in good form.'

'That's great.'

He frowned as he studied her. 'Why wouldn't you have a word with him?'

'Because it was a man-to-man moment.'

'I wonder what that means? . . . He's going to ask for an extra exeat because I've returned home.'

'Unlike his father, never one to miss an opportunity!'

'I'm missing something?'

'Since you have to ask, obviously not.'

'You misunderstand. I have a problem. Before or after I open the Veuve Clicquot?'

'The answer has to be one or the other, not both?'

'Damned be the puritan whose passion is a stranger to his imagination.'

Penfold buttered a piece of toast, coated it with lime marmalade. 'Inside, it always astonished me how good the coffee was, since institutional coffee is the butt of every comic's jokes. Which is a lead into asking if there's any more?'

'At least one cup, maybe two,' she answered.

He passed her his cup and saucer. 'It's strange, isn't it, how memory's triggered? When I lifted up my breakfast mug of coffee, almost invariably I'd visualize this room, right down to the missing piece of moulding we've always been going to replace, yet never have. Memory is a clever torturer. I used to lie in my bunk at night and . . . To hell with what I remembered. All that's over and done with.'

165

'You don't think . . . Well, if you talked about things, it could exorcize all those beastly memories?'

'Perhaps. But they have their purpose. They make the present that much sweeter . . . I thought I'd ring one or two agents and find out what jobs are going.'

She passed him the refilled cup and saucer, watched as he helped himself to two level teaspoonfuls of sugar. 'Wouldn't it be more sense for you not to do anything for a while and enjoy a complete break? We could go somewhere – Paris maybe.'

'Because it's spring?'

'You need to have time to relax.'

'Possibly. But the harsh fact is, I haven't been earning for more than three years and you've had this place to run and school fees to meet. Have we any savings left?'

'Some.'

'Meaning very little?'

She said nothing.

'How have you managed?'

'By economizing. And there's the money Aunt Maude left me.'

'You've had to use that?'

'Some of it.'

'How much?'

'I don't know exactly. I've just . . . just kept things going and not worried how . . . I have to go shopping now if we're to have any lunch. Would you like to come along?'

'Thanks, but I'll stay and enjoy home, sweet home.'

He watched the Astra drive out on to the road. The police had returned the Jaguar whilst he had been in jail and it was now in the garage. He knew she wanted to get rid of it because of the past and, as it had not covered a large mileage and was virtually in prime condition, it should provide a good trade-in value, which would allow him to buy . . . He was thinking like a spendthrift fool. From what Lucy had not said, he was certain their finances were in a parlous state. Until he had a job it was the height of folly even to think about buying another car.

He went through to the study, sat, checked the number he wanted, dialled. The connexion was made almost immediately. 'Hullo, Pam; can I have a word with Sydney?'

'Who's speaking?'

'Is this the perfect secretary who recognizes a caller after a single spoken word?'

'Mr Penfold?'

'Better late than never!'

'One moment, please.'

Unusually, her manner had been formal. Had Bampton, a man who believed in standards, demanded she alter her casual, occasionally flirtatious manner which, to a male client, was an asset to the agency?

'Gavin,' Bampton said.

'Morning, Sydney. How go things?'

'Could be worse, I suppose.'

'There speaks the eternal optimist . . . I gather there are still firms that understand security isn't a waste of time and money, only a threat to bonuses.'

'There are a few with directors of sufficient intelligence, yes.'

'That's good, because I'm looking for a job.'

'I see.'

'Is there a problem?'

'I'm sure you'll understand . . .' Bampton became silent.

'What am I to understand?'

'That . . . to put it bluntly, you've been away from the market for some little time.'

'Euphemistically put . . . I've been in jail, yes, but not for financial reasons.'

'Employers like . . . You must understand.'

'I was innocent and the evidence I gave in court was the truth.'

167

'Of course, of course. But employers . . .'

'What are you so reluctant to say? That they are often mindless? But they seldom remember much and my trial was over three years ago; in any case, it gained only a scintilla of national publicity because there was no sexual content. My name won't mean a thing today.'

'That might be right. But a security check is bound to turn up your . . . your stay.'

'Full security checks cost money, which lessens profit. Consequently, there are very few full security checks.'

'Your CV must show a gap in years that would have to be explained.'

'I took a long sabbatical in order to gain the several advanced qualifications I possess.'

'Dates would show that to be unlikely.'

'Dates can be altered.'

'I'm sorry, Gavin, that you should suggest I would be party to such deception.'

'The *verray, parfit gentil knyght.*'

'How's that?'

'An irrelevance. Where's the harm in altering the dates? It's not as if I would be trying to claim qualifications I haven't earned.'

'It would be unethical.'

'Sydney, I need a job yesterday, so ethics have to take a short holiday.'

'I'm sorry, but I'm afraid that isn't possible. Goodbye.' The line went dead.

Penfold slowly replaced the receiver. In view of the past, he had expected Bampton to help; he should have accepted that success had many fathers, failure was an orphan.

Three further phone calls, to three agents who had once been very happy to have him on their books, convinced him that while the general public would not have noted his conviction, the computer world most certainly had. Twice the receptionist had, after a pause, said that her boss was not in the office; the third time, the agent had spoken to him and bluntly said not to bother him again.

He went through to the sitting room and poured himself a gin and tonic. As he raised the glass, he was reminded of words Lucy had spoken when he had been drinking heavily. It was an illusion to believe alcohol could solve anything. There were times when an illusion was welcome. He drank.

As he poured himself a second drink, he understood something. Before he had gone to prison, he would not have considered altering the details of his CV, because that would have been dishonest.

Twenty-One

Lucy put the coffee machine on the stove. 'You're not forgetting we drive over to see Charles on Sunday? And – surprise, surprise – he's ordered his lunch!'

'I think we ought to find somewhere other than Chez Pauline to eat.'

'Why?'

'Isn't that all too obvious?'

'Gavin, my love, things will work out.'

'But in which way?'

'The wrong way, if you insist on attending your own funeral.'

'Thanks.'

'I'm beginning to think it's not sympathy you need, it's glasses. For heaven's sake, look at what we've still got: our health, a son . . .'

'Whose education is about to suffer.'

'I've told you, Father's said he'll pay the school fees. I know things are difficult . . .'

'Impossible.'

'They're going to improve. Something will turn up.'

'Will it, Mrs Micawber? Sorry. Yes, we still have more than most and I've become a miserable old fart.'

'Being a lady, I would not have used that expression, but in principle, I agree . . . Which is why we're going to blow away the shadows. It's a lovely day and if we find somewhere facing south that's protected from the wind, we'll be warm enough.'

170

'What are you proposing? A day as naturists?'

'A picnic. I'll nip out to M and S and buy something to make sandwiches and one of their sinful trifles covered with whipped cream; you can bring up a bottle from the cellar – didn't you say you still had four bottles of Romanée-Conti?'

'For a picnic? That's absurd.'

'Which is why that's what we'll drink.'

'The logic escapes me.'

'Good. The logical is usually deadly dull . . . Where shall we go?'

'Why not Fingal's Cave?'

'You almost smiled! I'll just nip out and get the food, then we'll be off.'

After she'd driven away, he brought up a bottle of Pommard from the cellar – there were certain limits to absurdity which a man had to observe. He put this on the kitchen table, picked up the day's copy of *The Times*, went along to the library and sat. Fifteen minutes later, he read the report of a robbery and rape and felt as if he'd just swallowed dynamite.

As the Astra drove in, he hurried through the kitchen and into the yard. Lucy stepped out of the car. 'The bag's are on the back seat.'

'You're never going—' he began.

'I bought smoked salmon, duck pâté, and gruyère cheese for the sandwiches, and since the object is to be totally sybaritic, a trifle for each of us. They're in a separate bag, right way up, so there's no need to get them out.'

'Come into the kitchen.'

'Where else d'you think I'm going to make the sand-wiches? . . . Gavin, you look . . . I don't know what you look. Has something happened?'

'It has.'

'What? Please God, not something nasty.'

'Quite the opposite.'

171

Jeffrey Ashford

In the kitchen she came to a halt by the table and said, as he put down the plastic bag he'd carried in, 'Well?'

'Read page four, column three near the bottom.' He picked up the newspaper and handed it to her.

She turned the pages, read. After a while, she put the newspaper down. 'Does that mean . . . mean that if they hadn't driven into the woman in Oak Cross, they'd have come here and maybe . . .' She stared at him, her expression shocked and fearful.

He held her tightly. He knew such selfishness was heinous, but he was thankful Alec had imagined himself to be a Grand Prix driver and as a result had knocked Mrs Lynch flying, thereby ensuring the original plan had had to be abandoned.

Penfold walked into the front room at divisional HQ and crossed to the desk.

'Can I help you?' the duty PC asked.

'I'd like a word with Mr Ingham.'

'I'm afraid he's no longer here – been transferred to county HQ.'

'Then with someone in CID.'

'I'll see who's free. Your name, please?'

'Penfold.'

'Would you take a seat?'

He sat on the padded bench and was annoyed and ashamed to find his hands were shaking: the uniform, the air of authority, were all too familiar . . .

Myers came through a doorway, saw him and crossed. 'You're out, then?' was his uncouth greeting.

'On Monday.'

'So what do you want here?'

'To ask you to read something in this paper.'

'Why?'

'Because it will convince you that from the beginning I was telling the truth.'

172

'Didn't know *The Times* was publishing fiction,' Myers said with a clumsy attempt at sarcasm.

Penfold opened the paper, folded the two halves back on each other, passed it across, indicating the article.

Myers read, looked up. 'Is that it?'

'Yes.'

He passed the paper back.

'Are you trying to say it's not germane?'

'If I knew what you're getting at, I might be able to answer.'

'They box in the car of the owner with their two cars; they tie him up and ram him into the back well on the drive to his home. Are you saying there's no connexion? Criminals repeat their method of crime, don't they?'

'If it's successful. Your history tried to say it wasn't. And as I remember things, you're some sort of computer operator. This bloke owns a very high-class jeweller's. Don't seem to be much similarity there.'

'Because you don't want to see it?'

Myers shrugged his shoulders.

'You always did your best not to believe me, didn't you?'

'That never took much effort. I've work to do – work that's important,' he added with aggressive rudeness.

'I want to speak to the detective inspector.'

'Not in the station.'

'When will he return?'

'Can't rightly say.'

'Then I'll return later on. Hopefully, he'll be able to employ a modicum of imagination.'

'Suit yourself, only I doubt there's anyone with even half the imagination you need.' Myers walked away.

As Penfold drove into the garage, Lucy hurried out of the house. 'Well?' she asked, her voice high with excited expectation as she met him near the gate.

'There's a new detective inspector and he wasn't there, so I had to speak to Myers – the detective constable who was always objectionable.'

'But even so, surely he could understand?'

'Refused to open his mind to the possibility. I said I'd return and speak to the inspector, but is he going to be just as biased?'

Kendrick, no longer an aide but a full member of CID, entered the general room and crossed to Myers's desk. 'Is that right, Mr Penfold was in earlier?'

'And if he was?'

'He's not on bail and reporting, so what brought him in?'

'To offer a cock-and-bull story he was soft enough to expect me to swallow. His kind never thinks the likes of us can have any bloody intelligence.'

'He could sometimes be right.' Since Myers's opinion of his ability no longer had any bearing on his career, Kendrick did not bother to simulate a respect for the other's age and experience. 'What's the story?'

'He'd read about a jewellery heist and rape up in Heighworth.'

'How can that concern him?'

'Tried to make out it showed all the balls he'd talked was true.'

'And did it?'

'Give over.'

'Come on, tell. How does nicking some jewels and raping a woman do him any good?'

'The owner of the jeweller's set off in his car, got boxed in by two other cars; masked men grabbed him, shoved him down in the well of his car, drove to his home, grabbed his wife and said if he didn't co-operate, they'd rape her, but if he did as they said, she'd be left alone. He went back to the shop, neutralized the alarm and opened the safe for them. They nicked stuff valued at over a million quid because some of it was meant to go into an exhibition. The police arrived and freed him after his wife had raised the alarm. The two who'd stayed in the house had raped her before they cleared off.'

'Bastards . . . Dave, it's got to be the same crew; apart from the rape, it's the same MO.'

'As naive as ever! Can't you see? Penfold read the report and thought we'd be soft enough to believe it helped him.'

'What's the description of the mob?'

'Wasn't one in the newspaper report.'

'So how about getting on to someone in Heighworth and finding out what they can tell us?'

'I've better things to do.'

'I haven't.'

'What is it with you? Think he's going to have you in for a booze-up if you suck hard enough?'

Kendrick crossed to his desk, used the internal directory of police phone numbers to find the one he wanted, and spoke to a desk sergeant at Heighworth.

'So?' Myers said, as Kendrick replaced the receiver. 'Now you can forget Penfold's nonsense?'

'They've only vague, useless descriptions. But one of the two rapists was called Bert. Penfold said one of the men in his car was called Bert.'

'Hardly an unusual name.'

'But one coincidence too far. The guv'nor ought to know.'

'Bother him with this nonsense and he'll have you doing paperwork for the next month. Anyway, Penfold said he'd be back to talk to him, so you can leave it to him to tell that ex-con where to go.'

'He wasn't here when Penfold was sent down, so he won't know all the details.'

'Lucky man.'

Park was large and slow-moving but far from slow-thinking; in style, an old-fashioned detective, first-class in the streets, second-class at the desk, third-class at keeping within budget. His belief that it was more important in practical terms to

175

defeat crime than to balance the books ensured he would gain no further promotion before retiring.

He looked across his desk at Penfold. 'On the contrary, I fully appreciate all you've said.'

'But don't accept it because I've been inside,' Penfold said bitterly.

'I like to think I am not so prejudiced.'

'You've told me one of the villains was called Bert. One of the men who grabbed me was called Bert. That means nothing?'

'You claim, I think, that the known facts of the theft in Heighworth are so similar to those in your case, the same mob must have been involved; that this, in turn, proves you were telling the truth. But you have to accept that it was never confirmed your car was in fact boxed in by two others, that you were blindfolded, gagged and wedged in the well when the car was driven by someone else and it hit the victim, that you were forced to drink heavily in order to make your version of events seem nonsense. The verdict of the jury has to be seen as showing that they did not believe you.'

'If I was lying at my trial, how d'you explain the fact that my lies of over three years ago are matched in the jewel robbery?'

'You may be choosing only later facts which match your version of the earlier case.'

'Check my court evidence.'

'Another possibility is coincidence.'

'If there's no connexion, the similarities would constitute a miracle, not a coincidence.'

'Service in the police force makes one realize that life could be described as one long coincidence.'

'Even to the extent that in each case one of the gang is called Bert?'

'How many hundreds of criminals are called Bert?'

Penfold stood. 'I've obviously been wasting your time. You may not be prejudiced, but you find it too difficult to accept that the police and court were wrong and I was innocent . . . I'm sorry to have bothered you.'

'Mr Penfold, yesterday Detective Constable Kendrick spoke to me about you. Because of what he told me – and because of his forthright expression of the possibility of your having been wrongfully convicted – I have spoken at some length to the officer in charge of the Heighworth investigations. He could tell me little more than you have read in the paper. For the moment there are no suspects.'

'And until there are, I've no chance of proving my innocence?'

'To be frank, even then it would not be easy for you to do so. Lacking the emergence of further evidence in your case – which after more than three years must be accepted as unlikely – to persuade the Court of Appeal your conviction was unjust, one of the Heighworth mob would have to admit to having taken part in your abduction. Why should he, when his mouthpiece tells him the near-impossibility of this being proved without his confession? Added to which, if he was the driver, he would not make an admission that would subject him to further serious charges; if not the driver, he wouldn't want to be a grasser.'

They sat in the priest's room. The television was on, but the sound was switched off.

'He just refused to help?' Lucy said bitterly.

'Give him his due, he didn't treat me as the ex-con I am, but he still hammered home the coffin nails. I'm beginning to know how Sisyphus felt every time he thought he was about to get the bloody marble to the top of the hill.' He was silent for a moment, then spoke with passion. 'Goddamn it, the bastards have to be identified and made to admit I was innocent. And if they don't want to talk, force it out of them.'

'I know how you feel . . .'

'Do you?'

'Yes, I do. But if there really is nothing more you can do,

wouldn't it be best just to accept life can be desperately unfair? If you become more and more angry and frustrated, what sort of state will you end up in? Can't we draw a line and leave the past in the past?'

'And all our money problems will be blown out of sight when I'm offered a top job by a philanthropic employer? The day I was banged up, Lucy, I learned how brutally unfair life is and I stopped believing there'd always be a fairy's wand to make everything right in the end.'

'But it would be so much better for both of us . . .'

He interrupted her. 'Christ! have I been slow. I've a better chance of identifying the villains who did the Heighworth job than ever the police will.'

Twenty-Two

It was a mean street, lined by small, mean terrace houses which abutted the pavement; in one or two cases an attempt had been made to introduce colour with window boxes, but a couple of smashed containers and spilled earth spoke of mindless vandalism. Only the cars, few of them old, parked on either side of the road showed it was not poverty that fostered the drabness – merely the lack of will to lead a more constructive life.

Penfold left the Astra, crossed the narrow pavement and knocked on the door of number 42. It was opened by a woman who stared at him with sharp suspicion. 'Are you Hazel?' he asked uncertainly. She had a pinched face, unkempt brown hair, a figure that went in and out at the wrong places, and her dress might have fitted someone else – hardly the woman of soaring passion in Ellis's letters.

She turned and shouted, 'Tom.'

'What's it bleeding well now?' came the answer through an opened doorway.

'Get here.'

Ellis appeared in the doorway. He stared at Penfold with surprise, even shock.

'Hullo, Ratty,' Penfold said.

Ellis swore.

'D'you know him?' she asked.

'Course I do.'

'Then what's he want?'

'How do I sodding well know?'

Since he hadn't yet been invited in, Penfold stepped into the tiny hall.

'Who is he?' she asked, as if Penfold had not been present.

'Him and me was inside together. I told you – had to learn him everything.'

She studied Penfold with sharp brown eyes – her only attractive feature – and judged the cut of his suit. 'Don't look like he was ever inside.'

'Well he was. So bring us something to drink.'

'There ain't anything – not after you and George last night.'

'Then get to the pub.'

'I need bread.'

'I just give you a score.'

'That was last week.'

'No, it weren't.'

Penfold said, as he brought his wallet out of his inside coat pocket, 'I'd like to offer a celebratory drink, if I may?' He extracted three five-pound notes and held them out.

She looked at Ellis. He grabbed the notes and passed them to her. She brushed past Penfold and left.

'Didn't never expect to see you again, Johnny.'

'Friends should keep in touch.'

'Yeah, only . . .'

'Especially when one owes the other so much.'

'How d'you know I was here?'

'You told me you lived in Tellsbury.'

'Don't remember that.'

'And since you're on the telephone, the directory provided your address.'

Ellis fingered his nose.

'Shall we sit down somewhere?'

He led the way into the front room, which was over-burdened with heavy furniture that shone from constant polishing.

Penfold sat. 'I had a chat with the coppers yesterday.'

'Pressuring you, is they? Bastards never give over.'

'It was my choice. I spoke to the detective inspector.'

Ellis was clearly uncomfortable, even afraid. 'What d'you do that for?'

'To tell him I'd learned something that confirmed I was innocent of the job for which I'd been convicted.'

'You still talking like that, and to a split, when it was likely him what put you inside? You're a real head case.'

'He explained that without knowing the names of the mob who pulled the Heighworth job, there was nothing he or anyone else could do to help me.'

'That was a smart job,' Ellis said admiringly.

'Aren't you forgetting the wife was raped?'

'No, only . . . Well, it was a real smart job.'

Priorities differed. 'They used the same way of grabbing the husband as they used on me. That tells you something, doesn't it?'

'Does it?'

'It has to be the same mob. The take was around a million quid, so someone will be spending.'

'Likely.'

'The job would have taken a lot of long, careful planning, and so it's likely they're locals. Heighworth is quite close to here.'

'What are you on about?' Ellis asked nervously.

'If you listen hard, there's a good chance you'll learn who's started spending.'

'What if I does?'

'You give me names.'

'Are you asking me to grass?'

'To give me information that could enable me to prove my innocence.'

Ellis spoke bitterly. 'Learn you all I can so as you don't get chivved something nasty, and then you come here and ask me to grass.'

Penfold brought out his wallet once more. Despite everything, he was prepared to gamble heavily, because the stakes were so high. He brought out a fifty-pound note.

'I ain't never been a grasser,' Ellis said, his beady eyes fixed on the money.

Penfold added a second fifty-pound note. 'Strike lucky and I'll be really generous.'

After a while, Ellis said, 'It ain't right, treating a broad like they did, is it?'

'Couldn't be more brutally wrong.'

'So it ain't really grassing to talk?'

'Far from it.'

Ellis reached forward and took the money.

March had come in like a lion and gone out like a lion: repeatedly, gales swept across the south, causing considerable damage; very heavy rain resulted in flooding and more damage.

The phone rang as Penfold stared out through the library window and wondered if the ancient oak beyond the lawn, damaged in the high winds, would finally fall despite the supports Hopkins had fixed before they had told him they could no longer afford to employ him even part-time. He picked up the cordless receiver.

'Is that you, Johnny?'

The voice was unmistakable. 'In one, Ratty.'

'There ain't no one listenin'?'

'Only me.'

'There's more dosh for names?'

'Provided the names are solid.'

'You sure there ain't no one else listenin'?'

'Quite positive.' There was a long pause. 'Are you still there, Ratty?'

'It ain't grassing, is it?'

'How could it be, when the information is for me, not the law?'

'Makes a difference, don't it?'

'All the difference.' Provided one forgot the use to which the information would be put. 'So what can you tell me?'

'There's three in the frame. Al Cullen, Ed Vince, Bert Ansell.'

'Eureka!'

'Weren't no mention of him.'

'When I was grabbed, Al was driving, Ed was the muscle and Bert gave orders . . . Who stayed in the house and raped the wife?'

'Can't say. Could of been them or someone I ain't heard.'

'Have you another name for Reg?'

'Can't say for sure.'

'Try a guess.'

'Ed's been seen with Reg Hobbs, only it don't seem likely it's the Reg what you wants.'

'Why's that?'

'He's big; wouldn't bother with the likes of you.'

'Unless he recognized I'm like the pineapple: my juice lies inside a rough exterior. Tell me about him.'

'You don't want to know.'

'On the contrary, I do.'

'Anyone troubles Reg Hobbs and it's concrete shoes.'

'He's hard?'

'Don't come no harder.'

'Known to the coppers?'

'Been after him for ever, but he's too bleeding smart for 'em. Runs a haulage firm as a front and the law don't never get past that and his mouthpieces.'

If Reg was as sharp as Ellis made out, then he was smart enough to have decided within a few blinks of the eyelids that if the police believed Gavin Penfold had run down Muriel Lynch when blind drunk, they'd dismiss his evidence as the wild story of a man desperately trying to avoid arrest; they would not ask themselves, if true, what job had been planned and why it had been so necessary to

183

try to hide the truth – could it be that, lacking any alarm, another attempt to break through a bank's security could be successfully mounted or the same modus operandi used in a different form of robbery?

'Thanks, Ratty.'

'You said there was extra bread.'

'I'll send you a cheque.'

'Ain't you learned bleeding nothing?' Ellis asked despairingly.

'It was a joke.'

He made it obvious he might have shared a cell, but not a sense of humour.

Penfold walked into the front room of divisional HQ and asked to speak to DI Park. After a brief call over the internal phone, the duty PC showed him into an interview room; ten minutes later, Park hurried in. 'Sorry to keep you waiting, but there's a lot on at the moment, so if you would keep things short.'

Penfold had stood, but Park did not shake hands; he sat once more. The DI remained standing. 'I've the names of three men who did the Heighworth job; I've a fourth name of the possible brains.'

'Really?'

'This is hard.'

'How did you learn the names?'

'A fellow ex-con told me.'

'Who is he?'

'You expect me to answer?'

Park finally sat on the opposite side of the table. 'Then it will be very difficult to place much credence in your information.'

'But still worth following up.'

'Perhaps.'

'I was inside, so I've sources of info you can't begin to tap. Proving my innocence will be no deal for you, but

nailing the bastards who raped Mrs Mansell and nicked a
million quid's worth of jewellery will be. That makes even
a doubtful whisper worth following up.'

'Since another force is handling the investigation, I can't do
anything beyond forwarding the information you give me.'

'You can add it's rock solid. That'll make certain they take
it seriously.'

Park reached across for the pad of paper and ball-point pen
to the side of the recording unit. 'What are the names?'

'Al Cullen, Ed Vince, and Bert Ansell. Reg Hobbs is likely
the brains.' As Penfold watched Park write, he enjoyed the
optimism that came from knowing the first move to prove
his innocence was finally being taken by the police.

Penfold was gardening – not something he enjoyed, but
without Hopkins the weeds were beginning to resemble
triffids – when a car drove into the yard. He jabbed the
hand fork into the stubborn earth, stood up from the kneeler
and began to walk. A man climbed out of the Rover saloon
who, when a dozen paces on, he identified as Park. They met
at the gate.

'Morning, Mr Penfold. I had to pass close by, so I thought
I'd call in and have a quick word.'

'Come on in.' He led the way round to the front door,
followed the other inside.

'You have a very attractive house,' Park said.

'We certainly like it.'

'How old is it?'

'Fifteenth century.'

'Extraordinary and heartwarming to see a house so old
remaining in such good condition.'

The stilted conversation should have warned Penfold, but
he desperately wanted to hear good news.

'I thought you'd like to know as soon as possible that I've
heard from Heighworth. Ansell, Cullen and Vince have been
questioned. Each of them strongly denied any knowledge

the jewellery robbery or rape of Mrs Mansell. When asked to provide alibis, they did so. These were found to be good.'

'Then they were ringed,' Penfold said heatedly.

'To quote the officer to whom I spoke, they were checked under a microscope, but they still held.' Park hesitated. 'Will you give me your word you will not repeat what I now tell you?' he finally asked.

'If you're ready to accept the word of an ex-con.'

'In your case, yes.'

'Then you have it.'

'The officer said that one of the names – he did not say which – had been spending heavily in a way that convinced them this man had been out on a rich job and therefore the alibi was probably false. But try as they might, they couldn't break it. Money or pressure is keeping tongues in line.'

'Then what's the next move?'

'Enquiries can't be taken any further.'

'Two of them raped the wife, so there has to be evidence; match the DNA.'

'The men wore condoms. In any case, DNA evidence on its own is insufficient.'

'There'll be other forensic evidence – hairs, fibres, stains.'

'Lacking the necessary evidence to apply for the authority to take samples and make searches, that's a non-starter.'

'How can there be the evidence you need before you search for it?'

'A question which all too often faces us.'

'Produce the evidence.'

'A polite way of saying, plant it?'

'Has no villain ever been fitted up?'

'One has to admit it can happen, but only when an officer is not only quite certain that the person concerned committed the crime in question, he is also ready to ignore the rules.'

'What about Reg Hobbs? Is his alibi equally unassailable?'

'He was staying in the property he owns in Italy and so

could not be questioned.'

'Check the records of his mobile phone and of the other three.'

'We lack the necessary authorization to do that.'

'Was the law made for the villains?'

'It sometimes seems so.'

'You're telling me the police can't do anything, and so I'm no nearer proving my innocence?'

'I'm afraid that is the position at the moment. There may, of course, be a lucky break in the future and you gain the evidence you need.'

'Would you bet on that?'

'I must leave.'

'Perhaps you should count yourself fortunate,' Penfold said bitterly, 'that the messenger who delivers bad news is no longer beheaded.'

'The detective inspector called in earlier,' Penfold said.

Lucy stared intently at him, her hand still gripping the plastic bag she had put down on the kitchen table. 'And?'

'The men have good alibis and no further enquiries will be made because the police lack the evidence to warrant these.'

'That's absurd. Can't they understand . . .'

'They understand their position perfectly, but not mine. If I'm left guilty and therefore unemployable and broke, that's my problem.'

She finally let go of the bag. 'We've no money left?'

'A figure of speech.'

'Is it? You've been poring over the figures. What do they really say?'

'We're just about to scrape the bottom of the barrel,' he admitted bitterly.

'Then what . . .' She moved until she could lie her cheek against his. 'Things will work out, my love.'

When this wasn't a Hollywood epic?

* * *

187

He awoke in the middle of the night and, inevitably, the worries of daylight returned, greatly magnified. Very soon the bank was going to demand either a cap on their overdraft or the start of repayment of it. This would force them to decide. Their only major asset left was Alten Cobb. Did they remortgage and continue to live there, despite the running costs, gambling things must turn their way? Did they accept that he would never be able to prove his innocence, so that he would remain unemployed and their only logical action must be to sell, invest the proceeds, and live in whatever circumstances, however reduced, were then open to them? Must he write 'Failure' in his CV? Was there no way of avoiding the bitterness of defeat?

About to fall asleep, further questions jerked his mind awake. Prison had taught him that a successful villain's great problem was how to conceal the proceeds of his crime. He had to find a seemingly invulnerable system of protection. Achilles had believed himself immortal, but a spear had struck his heel, which had not been covered by the waters of the Styx. What if Hobbs's 'heel' was at risk to a computer's spear? At the Counties Bank he had learned most of the dodges used by people to hide or launder money, and virtually all of them involved the use of computers. Hobbs must have amassed a very considerable capital – perhaps including the proceeds of a later and successful raid on a bank, never generally acknowledged because the last thing any bank was willing to admit was that its security had been breached – and, needing to conserve this, had banked it somewhere abroad from where it could be transferred to the UK in amounts unlikely to arouse suspicion, or to another country – Italy – where black money was a natural part of life. He'd get in touch with Ratty again and they'd . . . Fantasies were harmless unless one started to take them seriously.

Twenty-Three

P enfold went through to the kitchen to meet Lucy on her return. 'Alan will drive Charles back around seven this evening, so you won't need to fetch him,' she said.

'He and Frank seem to get on very well together.'

'They do, this holiday. But if you remember, last holiday, Charles named Frank his bitter enemy and said if he had a ray gun, he'd zap him.'

'Like countries, yesterday's enemies are today's friends.'

'Let's hope this friendship continues longer than between some countries. When he's with Frank, Charles works off a head of steam and becomes slightly more rational. Heaven only knows how schoolmasters remain sane.'

'Many of them don't.'

'I'm late back because I carried on to see Mother and Father.' She fidgeted with one of the buttons on the cardigan she wore. 'I told them things weren't too bright.'

'I wish you hadn't.'

'I'm sorry, I know how you feel, but . . . Father said he'll meet the school fees as he's promised before, and if they can do anything more to help, they will.'

'How can he afford that?'

'If necessary, they'll take out a mortgage on the house.'

'No.'

'As he said, everything they have will be left to me, so it'll just be an early transfer.'

'I won't let him do that.'

'Is it pride speaking?'

189

'Maybe.'

'And that's so much more important than Charles's future?'

'If necessary, we'll take out a second mortgage on here.'

'Wouldn't it be much more sense to . . .'

He waited.

'Never mind,' she said dully.

He left the kitchen.

They watched the evening news on television, but he failed to appreciate what he was looking at because his mind was trying to answer the question: could a fantasy of the night remain harmless, yet become a feasible proposition in daylight?

'I think I'll go up north and have another word with Ratty,' he said at breakfast.

Lucy looked at him, her expression sharp. 'Why?'

'To make him understand how very important it is to find something that'll force the police to continue searching for evidence.'

'You told me there wasn't anything more they could do.'

'Our family motto is *Hope on, hope ever.*'

'You're not telling me the truth. You're going to do something desperate.'

'She thinks too much; such women are dangerous.'

'For God's sake, don't be stupid.'

'I won't.' Who could define stupidity? Certainly not the stupid.

Hazel opened the front door. Penfold waited for her to ask him in and when she did not, stepped inside.

'What d'you want?' she demanded shrilly.

'I've come to have a word with Ratty.'

'Didn't I say not to call him that?'

'Sorry. It's because—'

'I don't want to know. Why can't you leave him alone? You and him ain't the same. You wouldn't be here if you

didn't want something.' Her tone became pleading. 'He ain't
been out of the nick long and I don't want him back inside
and me on me own . . . Please.'

'There's no cause for you to worry.'

'Of course there bloody is . . . I was so hoping . . . He
ain't here. He's gone out.'

'Do you mind if I wait for him to return?'

'Of course I do.' She turned, went through a far doorway,
and slammed the door behind herself.

Twenty minutes later, Ellis entered the front room. 'Didn't
expect to see you, Johnny,' he said uneasily.

'I thought it would be better to speak to you directly than
over the phone.'

'There ain't nothing more to tell.'

'But there is something you can do for me.'

'Like I say . . .'

'I'm sure I'll find the information I need in Reg's house.'

'Jesus! You ain't . . . If you're thinking . . . Johnny, have
you gone total apeshit?'

'You're worried that breaking into his pad would be far
too big a job for you?'

Ellis's pride was challenged. 'There ain't a job what's
too big.'

'You're worried there just could be too many alarms?'

'Ain't an alarm I can't bundle.'

'Nevertheless, you reckon the house will be tighter than a
virgin's pride and joy and, despite all your skills, you have
to flab?'

'It ain't the job,' Ellis said resentfully. 'I could make it,
don't matter how it's ringed.'

'But you're worried?'

'Of course I is when it's Reg's place. I've said: no one
messes with him.'

'Which is why he won't expect trouble. And to make things
easy, he's not in this country.'

After a while, Ellis muttered, 'Who says?'

'A copper.'

'Then it's a bleeding lie.'

'Not this time. They wanted to hear his alibi, but couldn't, because he'd taken off to his villa in Italy. So there's nothing to worry about. You suss out the pitch . . .'

'I ain't doing it.'

'Not to help a cellmate?'

'No.'

'Then I suppose that's that. I do have the consolation of knowing your refusal is saving me a couple of Ks.'

'You mean . . . ?'

'That's what I thought the job would be worth.'

'Straight?'

'In cash and no jokes about cheques.'

'So what are you after?'

'The opportunity to get into his place and examine his computer.'

'Jeeze, you are total apeshit! If I was to go in, you think I'd have you along?'

'Why not?'

'When you ain't even blagged a pensioner's home?'

'Suppose I wear L-plates?'

After a while, Ellis said, 'How d'you know he's got a computer? Been asking, I suppose. So now there's someone knows you're interested, and when Reg learns, he'll suss who did his place and he'll . . . Don't you understand? The last bloke what got up his nose ended with a hook through his belly and it took him a day to die.'

'Before you become too dramatic, I haven't asked anyone any questions to find out what's in his place.'

'Then how d'you know?'

'The law of probability. You tell me he's big and successful and in the rackets. So he earns big money and that creates a problem. What does he do with it? Doesn't want it lying around in cash because he'll grow ulcers worrying the house will be swooped by the law or it catches fire; he doesn't deposit it in a high-street bank because it'll make them curious and they'll tell the law that there's someone making more money than a footballer, so what balls is he kicking? He'll be using a computer.'

'You're trying to say he'll keep all his bread in one of them things?'

Penfold was careful not to smile. 'The money will be held in an offshore bank, sited in one of the countries where the staff have their curiosity removed by lasers. He'll use the computer to direct the offshore bank to transfer money to where he wants it and in small enough packets not to arouse anyone's curiosity – as often as not, through the haulage firm he runs. Nothing like a legit company for camouflage.'

'How d'you know all this?'

'Through my job.'

'Then you've done yourself real good?'

'Regretfully, no. I've always suffered the financial disability of honesty.'

There was a silence, which Ellis finally broke. 'There can't be no knowing who's in the house.'

'A good judgement has to be that he will prefer to have his secrets guarded electronically rather than by humans who might decide that while the cat was away, the mice would play. But if the job's well cased, we'll know for sure.'

'Suppose you're wrong? I ain't no hatchet man.'

Except from behind.

'I don't like it. She don't want me to do no more blagging.'

'Treat her to luxuries until she forgives you.'

'She don't change easy.'

'No woman can resist Gucci.'

'Two grand?'

'That's the deal.'

'I'd need gear that'll cost.'

'The necessary cash will be provided.'

'Ain't no need to let on to her what's happening.'

'Of course not.'

'She don't understand.'

'Eve's eternal problem.'

'Her name's Hazel.'

'Of course; my apologies.' Penfold stood. 'I'll phone tomorrow to learn when and how we move.'

'Still ain't learned a sodding thing,' Ellis said angrily. 'This ain't being done quick because it's got to be done good. I won't know nothing certain for a while. And if I sees him, I'm out.'

'He won't return until he's certain the law's stopped pressing. And in any case, who'd willingly quit the sun for wind and rain?'

Twenty-Four

Penfold waited until Lucy had driven off, then phoned. He was grateful Ellis answered the call and not Hazel. 'What's happening?'

'I've been using me brains.'

Potential bad news? 'And the result?'

'There's no one living there.'

'So it won't be difficult?'

'You don't know nothing! The firm what does the security has set up the alarms real smart. There ain't a window or door what's clear, and walk around inside and they're sounding. Try cutting 'em and you're fingered because they're electronically questioned all the time and if they don't respond, the control rooms knows and rings the coppers to tell there's trouble.'

'Then how do you silence them?'

'There ain't no way.'

'I thought you said there wasn't a system you couldn't fix?'

Ellis chuckled. 'There's times you ain't as smart as me, Johnny.'

'Many more. But surely if you can't silence the alarms, the job's off?'

'You don't silence 'em, you set 'em off.'

'I have the feeling that we're talking on crossed wires.'

'The front door will be bolted – always is. But there has to be another door what ain't so solid on account of not being able to bolt it before you leaves, so that'll just be secured with locks and there ain't a lock I can't twirl. So now do you get it?'

'No.'

'You don't know nothing.'

'My education has been very narrow.'

'I unlocks the back door and opens it. I watch how long before the alarms go off – that says the time there is for someone to get to the control box and feed in the code. When they goes off, I shut the door and lock it and scarper. The coppers arrive, find everything solid and no windows bust, so they thinks it's a false alarm. But they calls for the key-holder, who's a mate of Reg, and when he opens up, they go inside, he switches off the alarm what's been annoying everyone, and they search. They find nothing, so they leave.

'The next day, there's blokes from the security firm along what tries to work out what's wrong and don't find nothing because there ain't anything to find. That night, I does the same thing again. When the coppers find there's still nothing, they shout and say that one more false alarm and they're not interested. The security firm comes back and still don't find the trouble.

'I do it again, this time staying inside with the door locked and when the coppers find nothing outside, they say that's it and they can't be bothered to look inside and the alarms can ring all bleeding night as far as they care. People can't remember numbers, so I looks around the control box and find a bit of paper stuck in a corner with numbers on it and when I tap 'em in, the alarms stop . . . Smart, eh, Johnny?'

Had Ellis read about the boy who shouted wolf so often that when one really threatened him, his cries were ignored and he was eaten? 'Much smarter than I could ever be.'

Ellis was gratified by the praise. 'Can't all be the same, can we?'

'So now we move?'

'It don't make no sense for you to come in. You says what you want and I brings it out.'

'I have to work the computer and check the files on it.'

'Forget it, Johnny. I go in on me own.'

'Isn't the bonus worth a little risk?'

'You ain't said nothing about a bonus.'

'I must have forgotten.'

'How much?'

'If things go as I hope, you can use your imagination.'

Ellis swore. Penfold was unable to judge whether that was an expression of greedy expectation or of annoyance at his own weakness.

Four days later, sitting on the front seat of a Ford Focus that Ellis had 'borrowed', Penfold stared at the front of number 56. When he'd first seen the detached Edwardian house, one of twenty similar buildings in the road, he had expressed his surprise that Hobbs, if so successful, should live in a modest – many would say dowdy – home. His comment had aroused Ellis's scorn. Couldn't he yet understand that a smart villain did nothing that would give the coppers the chance to worry him? – it was only the punks who flashed their wealth. And if Hobbs had a place in Italy, likely that was where he spent real bread; likely it was a palace with gold taps in the bathrooms . . .

A light in a downstairs room went on. 'There's someone in the house,' Penfold said, nervous excitement causing his voice to rise.

'Ain't you heard of lights what are switched on with a timer to make suckers think there's someone about?'

'How can you be certain . . .'

'Think I didn't check?'

The more obvious his tension, Penfold thought, the less willing Ellis was going to be to be accompanied by him. But the currency of cowardice was imagination. Despite the late hour, he could not stop surmising that in one of the other houses someone might have looked out and noticed two men sitting in a car and thought that sufficiently suspicious to ring the police.

'Got your gloves on?'

'Yes.'

'Come on, then.'

As he left the car and followed Ellis – who carried a small, heavily laden hold-all – across the road, he wondered if underneath the other's apparent calm there was nervous fear similar to that which churned his stomach.

The side gate squeaked and to him it sounded with the force of a clap of thunder. They walked along the narrow path, between the house and the six-foot-high fencing, and around to the back door. The new moon was all but obscured by cloud, but the loom of town light prevented total blackness and the bulks of the houses beyond the garden were discernible. Someone, unable to sleep, might be looking through a window and notice two patches of moving blackness . . .

Ellis brought out his twirlers, lock-picking instruments that looked like oversized dentist's probes. Swearing continuously – his way of easing tension – he worked with one after another until he forced the top lock. That done, he forced the lower lock. He opened the door and led the way inside, switched on a torch whose bowl had been partially covered to reduce the size of beam. Penfold followed and, made clumsy by fear, tripped on the sill and fell sideways against the wall. He blundered into something that crashed to the floor.

'Why don't you just bleeding well bell the coppers and tell 'em to come along?' Ellis said, as he hurried along to a small alcove in which was the alarm control box. He tapped in six numbers and waited, body tensed. As the silence continued, he relaxed. He pushed past Penfold, shut the outside door and locked it.

He led the way up the stairs, which had a half-landing to provide a ninety-degree turn. There were four bedrooms and two bathrooms. One of the bedrooms had been turned into an office and on a large utilitarian desk were a tower, VDU screen, printer and disk holder. Ellis drew the curtains and switched on the overhead light, causing Penfold to suffer a moment of breath-catching fear before he remembered the time switches that ensured there would always be at least one room illuminated.

He sat in front of the computer, switched it on.

'I'll blag the peter.' Ellis crossed to the far wall, swung out a large print to reveal the door of a safe. 'Ain't no better than a tin box,' he said with contempt.

As Penfold worked the computer, searching for a lead to the offshore bank account he was convinced would be on file, Ellis opened the hold-all and brought out a small, high-powered electric drill, several bits made of special steel, and a sectional jemmy, one end of which was pointed, the other chisel-shaped. He plugged the drill into a wall socket, fitted a bit and slowly – three bits were blunted before he succeeded – drilled a hole in the upper corner of the safe door. He inserted the point of the jemmy into the hole, and using all his strength – greater than his form suggested – sweating, swearing when he failed to gain sufficient purchase, alternately applied pressure downwards and upwards.

Penfold opened another file, drew another blank. Just as Ellis was obviously finding the safe far stronger than a tin box, so it was beginning to look as if he might have been wrong to assume an offshore account hiding black money. The thirteenth, fourteenth, fifteenth files proved useless . . .

Ellis finally levered the edge of the front steel plate sufficiently clear to be able to reverse the jemmy and insert the chisel end. It took him only minutes to force a way inside and find the safe contained far less than he'd hoped. He surreptitiously pocketed a small bundle of fifty-pound notes.

Penfold looked up. 'What's in the safe?'

'Nothing.'

He stood, crossed the floor to look inside the shattered safe, saw papers, files and cheque books. Hoping the papers and files would give him the information he wanted, he brought them out, together with a cheque book that had become caught up between two files. He put them down on the desk, at the side of the computer, and quickly looked through them. There were no bank accounts – only past credit-card statements – and no references that could be followed up. The cheque book had been issued by the Counties Bank – something of an irony.

'Best be moving,' Ellis said.

'Not yet.' He returned to the computer, opened another file.

Time passed. Noticeably becoming nervously impatient, Ellis finally said, 'We can't stay no longer, Johnny.'

'I need more time.'

'Suit yourself, but I'm off.' Ellis picked up the hold-all and crossed to the doorway.

Would Ellis leave him, knowing the danger into which that would place him? Probably. *Sauve qui peut.* So he had to concede defeat. It had been foolish optimism to believe he could ever find the evidence he needed to prove his innocence. Hobbs had made certain his reputation and financial security were destroyed and could never be restored and his family was condemned to a future as bitter as the immediate past had been . . .

He switched off the computer, stood, and took two paces towards the doorway, then came to a stop. Revenge might be a kind of wild justice that should be weeded out, but it could soften bitterness. He returned to the desk, switched on the computer, picked up one of the credit-card statements to read the reference number.

'If you ain't coming . . .' Ellis began.

'Five minutes, Ratty, and not a second longer.'

'I ain't bleeding waiting.' But he remained by the doorway until Penfold once more switched off the computer. As they left, Ellis said, 'I ain't never blagging with you again.'

One could hardly blame him.

They parked in a back street, visually checked they'd left nothing, walked around the corner to the council car park in which were a dozen cars, including the Astra. Penfold opened the boot for Ellis to drop the hold-all into it, settled behind the wheel and started the engine. 'You're sure the alibis are fixed solid?'

'So long as I get the dosh to pay.'

'It'll be with you very soon.'

Penfold backed, turned, drove to the pay booth. The barrier was up and there was a notice stating that the automatic pay machine was out of order and drivers were asked to put the appropriate parking fee, as listed on the card behind the window, through the small flap in the door of the booth. Penfold opened the car door.

'Where you going?' Ellis asked.

'To pay the parking fee.'

Ellis was so astonished by this mindless stupidity that for once he was briefly silent.

Hazel met them at the front door. She ignored Ellis, faced Penfold. 'What d'you want now?'

'What d'you think he wants?' Ellis asked aggressively. 'Same as me: a bloody large drink.'

'He ain't coming in.'

'What you on about?'

'When you came out last time, you promised you wasn't doing no more jobs. Then he turns up and you've been screwing. You think I want to spend more nights not being able to sleep, wondering if you was nicked and would be inside and me on my own until I'm grey-haired and losing all me teeth? He ain't coming in, now, not never.' She folded her arms across her chest.

Hoping to assuage her anger, Penfold said, 'Tom's been—'

'A bloody fool because he ain't ever anything else. But he's my man and when he's inside, neither of us is alive. So

201

take yourself off to where you came from and don't mess
with the likes of us again.'

He hesitated, decided further words would only exacerbate
her anger, turned to walk back towards the car.

'Don't forget to burn the clothes,' Ellis said. 'And I'll need
the dosh quick.'

'We don't want your money,' she said fiercely.

'Don't be so bleeding daft.'

The argument was growing fiercer as Penfold reached the
parked Astra.

He stopped in Hilsden and crossed to a public call box,
dialled 999 and asked for the police.

'The owner of fifty-six Layton Road, Winchley, has child
pornography on his computer.'

'May I have your name and—'

He replaced the receiver. He returned to the car, drove
south once more. On his return from Italy, Hobbs would
be questioned by the police. When child pornography was
found on his computer, he would be arrested, charged, tried,
convicted and imprisoned. In jail, paedophiles were loathed
and treated to every possible humiliation; for a man who must
consider himself a criminal tsar, such humiliation would be
magnified many times by the knowledge that it was not he
who had downloaded the obscene images; but no one would
believe him, even though he spoke the truth.

That Lucy had not slept, had been haunted by black
thoughts, was evident from the tearful relief and irrational
anger with which she greeted his safe return.

Twenty-Five

I t was not until Wednesday that Penfold remembered something which he realized might offer what until then he
had accepted was beyond his reach: Hobbs banked with the
Counties Bank.

Because the police might investigate, because evidence on
a hard disk could only be completely erased by destroying the
disk, because normal and mobile phone calls could be traced
to source, he decided he dared not use his own equipment.
He drove to a computer centre in north London – where an
individual purchase for cash would be virtually untraceable
– and bought a bog-standard computer and printer; in south
London he bought a mobile that worked on pre-paid calls and
was on offer because it was old stock and provided none of
the latest must-have gismos.

Back at home, he began his search for the evidence that
would clear his name and restore his fortunes. Before he had
ceased to work at the bank, he had identified a major fault in
security and alerted management. Asked to devise a system
to eliminate this fault, he had done so; but because the work
would have cost considerable time and money to implement
and therefore affected other projects, threatening bonuses, it
had not been put into operation before he had left. Had it
been since then, he was now going to find it very difficult,
perhaps even impossible, to break into the bank's records.

He was gratified and relieved to find that staff bonuses
had remained more important than the security of customers'
accounts.

He studied Hobbs's private and company accounts: substantial credits were frequently paid into both, without a regular time rhythm, by a bank in the Cayman Islands; banks in those islands offered services well known to people who wanted their financial dealings unrecorded in their home countries.

Hacking into a bank was a long, boring, exasperating task, and if the security was good, probably fruitless. The company and its network had to be researched; the network where the computer was connected had to be mapped to know what was on the computer in question and the route required to reach that; access to the network had to be gained in order to launch an attack.

Research checked the domain name that provided the Internet protocol number of the network; mapping the target determined the network security measures in place (a delicate operation, as there might be security mechanisms which identified when the network was being scanned) and identified particular targets, such as the systems which held the accounts of customers. To obtain access, it was easiest to enter a 'public' service, then launch an attack on the 'private' service; having gained a foothold, an attack could be mounted against the target system.

Individual systems were usually protected by a basic password; Strong Authentication mechanisms were only used for high-risk systems and, in the case of banks, those which took a proper, sophisticated view of security. Security measures were Firewalls or Intrusion Detection Systems. The preferred method of attacking Firewalls was to locate and take advantage of 'holes' left by manufacturers, who were notorious for building systems with mistakes . . .

As he started work, Penfold sent a silent prayer to the gods of hacking that his target was not covered by the degree of security it should be.

On 8 May – almost a summer's day – Lucy entered the library, closed the door behind her. She came up to the desk. 'Two detectives are here,' she said, her tone fearful.

'Did they say why?'

'Just that Detective Inspector Park wants a word with you. The other one is that beastly man who always makes himself so objectionable . . . Gavin, what can they want?'

He stood. 'Nothing to worry about.'

'For God's sake, how can you say that? Not worry when police come here after . . .'

'It may be nothing to do with that.'

'What if it is?'

He put his arms around her.

'I'm so scared.'

'I know. Unfortunately, for us the police have become the less than reassuring presence they are for most. Where are they?' He released her.

'In the priest's room.'

'It'll be a good idea if you now disappear.'

'No.'

'The sight of both of us on tenterhooks might give the right impression.' He smiled. She did not smile back. He leaned forward and kissed her unresponsive lips, left, and made his way along the corridor.

As he entered, Park stood; true to form, Myers did not.

'I hope we're not interrupting anything?' Park said.

'I'm only doing a little research.' Irony had been met with irony. 'In any case, an interruption can be welcome when work isn't being successful . . . Do sit down. And may I offer you something to drink?'

'Thanks, but we won't.' Park sat. 'We're here because we've been asked by another force to make enquiries about an incident which occurred recently. You'll know to what I'm referring.'

'Will I?'

Park's manner was neutral. 'Do you remember telling me that you could identify the men who carried out the jewellery robbery in Heighworth and raped the unfortunate jeweller's wife?'

'Of course.'

'And I told you that even if the identification proved correct, it was very unlikely you would be enabled to prove your claimed innocence?'

'My innocence.'

'As you wish. I gained the impression you were determined to prove your case.'

'Is that surprising?'

'So determined, you were prepared to take any steps you thought might help you do that.'

'Provided they were legal, of course.'

'You are suggesting you would not consider doing anything illegal; you do not believe that the wrong you claim was done to you would warrant this?'

'I've always held that a hypothetical question deserves only a hypothetical answer.'

Myers was bored and annoyed; had he conducted the questioning, it would have been far more direct and robust.

'When you spoke to me at the station, you named Reg Hobbs as the man who had organized the jewellery heist. His house has recently been broken into.'

'Then dog really does eat dog.'

'His safe was forced. Papers that had been in it were on the desk and, judging from their appearance, had been read. Why would a casual burglar be interested in information seemingly of absolutely no use to him?'

'I've no idea.'

'Do you think he might have been searching for information relevant to your abduction and enforced drunkenness some years ago?'

'If you're suggesting, not very obliquely, it was I who broke into the house and forced the safe, you're overrating my illegal capabilities by many magnitudes.'

'Prior to the break-in, the ancient ploy of crying wolf was

used to overcome the alarm system – which was a very elaborate one. As you have, no doubt correctly, downgraded your housebreaking expertise, it would have had to be an accomplice who planned and executed the break-in, wouldn't it?'

'Supposition piled on top of supposition.'

'One of the men apparently used the computer. Why?'

'I don't know, but I'm certain you're about to suggest an answer.'

'Very well. He was hoping to uncover evidence which would assist his claim that he was innocent of the crime for which he had been imprisoned.'

'You seem very determined to inculpate me.'

'To elucidate the truth. The intruder who used the computer—'

'Wouldn't it save time to be specific?'

'You downloaded obscene material on to the computer, didn't you?'

'No.'

'Such material was on the hard disk and when Hobbs, who returned from Italy very recently, was questioned, he denied that he had ever downloaded such material and expressed his abhorrence of it.'

'Was he believed?'

'He found it impossible to prove the negative – that he did not download it – and so, since it was on his computer, he was charged. After a hearing before magistrates, he will appear at a crown court next month. Assuming that you were wrongly accused of a crime and left no way in which to prove your innocence, I imagine you must delight in the irony of having placed your tormentor in precisely the same predicament.'

'It is said that revenge is a dish that tastes even better cold than hot.'

'On the night of the break-in, a call was made to the police informing them that the obscene child images were on the computer. The informant cut the connexion before he could be asked to give his name and address and the source of his information. The PC who took the call was sufficiently intrigued that when logging it, he added the comment that the informant spoke with a cultured accent.'

'Surely a very politically incorrect description for a policeman to make?'

'All 999 calls are location-identified, and this one was made from Hilsden.'

'Is that in some way significant?'

'If you were driving from Winchley to here, you would almost certainly pass through Hilsden.'

'You are definitely accusing me of having broken into Hobbs's house?'

'Not until I am certain I know all the facts.'

'My experience is that that's unusual: the police are seldom interested in facts.'

'Facts are truth and we are always searching for the truth. Just as you were – the truth you believed would prove yourself innocent.'

'You allow me an innocent motive, then?'

'Which would not make the illegal act legal – any more than evidence of Hobbs's financial dealings would be likely to prove your innocence.'

'Not if it could be shown he had wealth far beyond any that could be justified by his legal activities?'

'As I think I pointed out previously, only direct evidence favourable to you would succeed in establishing your innocence; and the unlikely event of this ever becoming available, since the giving of it would ensure the arrests of others . . . Where were you on the night of the twenty-first of this month?'

'At home, almost certainly. We seldom go out at night these days.'

'Your wife would also have been here?'

'Naturally.'

'Is there anyone else who would be able to corroborate that?'

'I've no idea if we had anyone to a meal. I'd have to check with Lucy – she has a much better memory than I.'

'Then perhaps you would ask her if you did have guests?'

Penfold left, returned four minutes later. 'As I said, she remembers, I forget. I wasn't here because that was the night of the reunion.'

'Which was held where?'

'Ronchester.'

'Who else was present?'

'Tom Ellis for one and three others whose names escape me.'

'Were any of them convicted criminals?'

'I should like to feel insulted by the question, but circumstances leave me without that privilege. I was in the same cell as Ellis for part of my sentence. The other three were friends of his, so I can't say what their social standing is, but I confess I wouldn't be surprised to learn they had form.'

'Seemingly, then, really only a reunion for the two of you.'

'Reunions have a habit of enlarging beyond their remit.'

'When did it end?'

'In the not-so-early hours of the morning.'

'And you returned here?'

'I stayed with Ellis and his charming lady friend. Had I returned by car, any second arrest for driving under the influence would have been fully justified.'

'I imagine the four men and the lady will confirm what you've just told me?'

'Since it's the truth, I certainly hope so.'

Park stood. 'You make an apt pupil, Mr Penfold.'

'Pupil?'

'You have forgotten that those you named as having carried out the Heighworth job were able to deny the accusation with unshakable alibis?'

'I'd call that a coincidence.'

'I am sure you would . . . Naturally, I will ask you for names and addresses and the persons concerned will be asked to verify your alibi . . . which I imagine they will.'

'To your frustrated annoyance?'

'Can two wrongs make a right? One would have to be a far keener moralist than me to know.'

After being given Ellis's name and address – Penfold admitted his memory was still adrift, but Ellis was sure to be able to provide the information concerning the others – Park said goodbye and left, followed by Myers, who looked even more disgruntled than usual.

As the car drove off, Lucy hurried downstairs. 'Well?

'They admitted defeat,' he answered. And left him defeated.

Twenty-Six

Penfold stared at the VDU and wondered why the hell he was continuing to hack into the bank's secrets. Before their visit, he had forgotten – deliberately? – Park's warning that it was most unlikely he would be able to prove his innocence by exposing Hobbs's financial dealings. Show Hobbs had wealth that could not be explained by business profits, yes; show these proved Hobbs had masterminded his abduction and subsequent guilt, that Al Cullen had been driving the car that had knocked Mrs Lynch to the ground, no. The hours he had already spent at the computer, the many more needed to gain success, were a folly . . .

Yet at least when he was probing the bank's defences, calling on all his skills and knowledge gained from anti-hacking courses, he was not thinking about the future – the disappearance of a comfortable life, the sale of Alten Cobb (which Lucy now agreed was inevitable), applying for jobs and being refused, the frustrated bitterness of knowing he was a victim of injustice . . .

On 22 July, he finally broke into Hobbs's account with the Batono Bank. Four million one hundred and twenty-four thousand dollars and fifteen cents. He giggled at the fifteen cents, because he was feeling light-headed, as one could when a long, hard task was finally accomplished.

He was sorry Lucy wasn't at home to share his success, however fruitless; she was out, ferrying Charles to friends for lunch. He made his way to the sitting room, where he poured himself a gin and tonic – his first drink for a long

while because, in the name of economy, they had rationed
alcohol almost out of existence. Glass in hand, he returned
to the computer. As he stared at the screen, it became
blank. Very appropriate, he thought; a reflection of life. The
previous month, Park had called to tell him Hobbs had been
sentenced to five years in jail. Park had not referred to the
coincidence, correctly assuming that this could only engender
more bitterness: guilt and innocence were indistinguishable
– but, of course, only superficially. He had left prison much
poorer than when he had gone in; Hobbs would leave it richer
because of the interest his capital would have earned. He
drained the glass; the gin and tonic might have been water
for all the pleasure it had given him.

As he reached for the mouse and brought the screen back to
life, he recalled Ellis's scorn when, after the break-in, he had
paid a parking fee even though that could easily and safely
have been avoided – in Ellis's eyes, only a fool was honest
when there was no risk in being dishonest . . .

Hobbs's money was in the Batono Bank because it was the
profit of crime and had to be hidden from the authorities in
Britain. So were it to disappear, into another offshore account
about which he could know nothing, he could not complain
about his sudden poverty without incriminating himself; and
even if he did complain, who would be able to trace the
money's whereabouts?

At the end of August, Kendrick hurried into the CID general room.

'The guv'nor's been shouting for you,' Myers said. 'Been
away so long, you've forgotten you're meant to start work
before the day's half over?'

Kendrick crossed to his desk, sat. 'You're lucky to see me
come back before next year . . . It was really great. Not a
cloud in the sky and the sea as warm as toast the whole time
we were there. Margery said that's where we're going on our
honeymoon and no arguing. As I said, Who's arguing?'

'When's the marriage?'

'Next spring.'

'Gives her time to come to her senses.'

Park entered, came to a halt in front of the first row of desks. 'Finally arrived, then? You look as if you had a good holiday?'

'Couldn't have been better, sir.'

'And now you're keen to get back to work?' His tone was lightly sarcastic. He dropped two folders on the nearest desk. 'As quick as you like with the witness statements. And make sure Vyans is positive what colour bomber jacket his assailant was wearing.' He turned and left.

Kendrick stood, went forward and picked up the two folders, then remained where he was. 'Something odd happened when we were having a drink at a café overlooking the beach.'

'Yeah?'

'I saw a couple walking along the road that rings part of the bay. Guess who they were?'

'The chief constable and his prune of a wife.'

'Mr and Mrs Penfold. He recognized me and came across to talk.'

'Hope you kowtowed.'

'They were both really friendly, which seemed odd, considering all that's happened. Even invited us to his hotel for drinks. Guess what that was like?'

'Is this a goddamn guessing game? How am I supposed to know?'

'A real luxury pile. And he and his missus had a suite almost as large as a house. We were in the sitting room and champagne and some eats were brought up by a waiter. What did that cost! . . . Real odd, him obviously loaded, considering it seemed he must have been skint after being inside.'

'Him skint? Be your age. Lives a life of luxury on all he and his ancestors have stolen from the likes of us.'

Kendrick laughed.

'What's so funny?'

'Your hang-ups. Just can't accept, can you, that's he's the kind of man who won't even have nicked a tube of Smarties when he was in shorts?'